SAMMY'S RED SHIRT

LOST BOY, HOMELESS GIRL

By

Reva Jo Gordon

To order, call 1stBooks Library at 1(888) 280-7715

This book is a work of fiction. Places, events, and situations in this story are purely fictional. Any resemblance to actual persons, living or dead, is coincidental.

ISBN: 1-4033-6885-6 (e-book)
ISBN: 1-4033-6886-4 (Paperback)
ISBN: 1-4033-6887-2 (Dust Jacket)

Library of Congress Control Number: 2002111811

This book is printed on acid free paper.

Printed in the United States of America
Bloomington, IN

1stBooks - rev. 03/06/03

Acknowledgements

Inspiration: Patrick, Leah, Andrew, and Brent.

In deep appreciation, I thank the following for their encouragement, assistance, or willingness to read my manuscript. Gordy, Gary, Jennifer Gordon, Gloria, Tom, Leah Zuber, LaVona Rodgers, Lavena Nickerson, Lora Popovich, Barbara Cummings, Bonnie Foster, Lavesta Vance, Lorine Stewart, Rosie Brickey, Rev. R. Dean Goodwin, Maxine Mindling, Rev. James Schofield, Martha Beyerly, Don and Sue Schaffer, Karen Colonna, Nathan Householder, Kilian LaFraniere, Patrick O'Brien, Violette Hunter, Shirley Kelly, Mark Calvert, Sheila Lewis, Sue Springsteen, Jane Dodge, Tracy Owen, Sue Young, Dean Bemis, Mary Ann Loode, Diane Newburg, Paul Bagdon, Dr. Doris Hammond and especially Tom Rohrer of the Genesee District Library who answered many reference questions and Sandra Rundell who spend hours editing this book.

Dedication

To Roland K. Gordon

My husband, my friend,

my confidant, my love.

Chapter One - Saturday Morning

Saturday when Sammy slammed an old board into a big cow pie at his grandparent's farm and splashed fresh, stinking manure all over Perfect Prissy Sibyl, he felt really good!

Watching his 13-year-old cousin try to wipe big splatters off her crisp, white shorts, red and white shirt, and white shoes with red shoelaces caused almost six-year-old Sammy to giggle. When Perfect Prissy Sibyl blinked trying to see around the big gob on her round, dark rimmed glasses, Sammy couldn't help it. He laughed long and loud.

The more Sibyl tried to wipe the manure off her arms, shirt and shorts, the more she got manure on her hands, and the louder she screamed. And the more Sammy laughed! Soon Sibyl's and Sammy's parents came running out of the farmhouse closely followed by their grandparents.

Uncle Howard and Aunt Bertha went right to their precious daughter and made soothing noises. Uncle Howard took his handkerchief out of his back pocket and made a face as he tried to

1

wipe manure off Sibyl's face and arms. Aunt Bertha closed her eyes and squealed "Yuck," as she wiped her daughter's clothing with a couple of Kleenexes.

"He did it. Sammy did it," Sibyl screamed pointing at Sammy. He still could not keep a smile off his face so covered with freckles that he looked like he had been sprinkled with small dots of sticky, butterscotch pudding.

"Sammy Hendricks!" His father Larry grabbed Sammy's upper arm and jerked him toward the house. Sammy quit smiling but glanced at his mother and wondered if she was hiding a smile behind her hand.

"You knew we only stopped by to help your grandparents move their bedroom furniture. Why did you go to the pasture?" his father demanded, as he marched him through the kitchen.

"Sibyl told me there was an elephant out there, and we should go see it. I looked and looked for it out there. When I asked where it was, Precious Prissy Sibyl said there wasn't any elephant. She said I was stupid and dumb 'cause I thought there was. So I splashed her." Sammy bent his head to one side. "That uh, manure really got on her, didn't it?"

"You're right on the east edge of becoming a brat, Sammy," his father's voice was stern. "You were bad to splash manure on Sybil. Now. sit in a chair in the basement until we get the furniture moved." Larry pushed him toward the basement door.

Sitting alone in the chair by the pool table, Sammy still felt good. He thought his granddad winked at him and believed his grandma almost laughed. His grandparents must know Sibyl was not as perfect as her parents thought. Grandma probably figured out that it was Perfect Prissy Sibyl who broke her favorite flowerpot on the porch.

Miss Perfect never got dirty. Dirt seemed to jump on Sammy's clothes as though his clothes and dirt were as attracted to each other as magnets. Yeah, Sammy knew he got dirty digging in the dirt of the flowerpot on the porch that day, but he didn't knock it over. When Sybil told their grandparents Sammy broke it, she lied.

That was just another of the mean things Sibyl did. She deserved to smell like... he must not say the bad word, but he could think it. With big letters! He grinned. Other than his name it was about the only word he could spell.

"Clinker Dab," he sighed after 20 minutes. "It's awful lonesome here in this ole basement. Tomorrow I will be good," he told himself.

He sat in the back seat of the family's blue Buick well behaved and quiet all the way home and kept the promise to himself. Then the bad telephone call came just as Emily prepared lunch. His father answered and had a sad look on his face when he finished the call. Sammy listened as his father told his mother that they would not be getting the baby.

Sammy stuck out his lower lip. "Not getting a baby sister? That's the only present I wanted for my 'bertday.'" He stamped his feet, grabbed a box of cheese crackers, and threw them in a corner.

"Hush," his mother said as his father explained that the birth mother had changed her mind and decided to keep the baby.

"You promised. You said I'd have a sister," Sammy stood in the middle of the green and white kitchen glaring at his parents. Sunshine flowed through the flowered curtains and made the small boy's Halloween orange colored hair even brighter. He did not know he had a bright rooster tail standing up at the back of his head. Tears sprang from his blue eyes, and rolled down over the butterscotch pudding colored freckles scattered across his rosy cheeks and short nose. He dug his eyes with his fist and sniffed loudly. "Clinker Dab! That's all

I wanted for my 'bertday.'" He sniffed loudly trying to keep the tears back but more rolled down his freckle-splattered cheeks.

"Don't cry. Come here, son." Larry, who had an identical cleft in his chin just like Sammy's, stretched out his hands.

Sammy wiped his nose and cheeks with his red knit shirtsleeve. He sniffed twice, then placed his small hands with their dirty nails in Larry's big ones and looked up at him.

"Your mother and I are disappointed, too. We're really lucky we had you before Mama had to have her operation. We really wanted a sister for you, Sammy. You know that."

Sammy pulled away. "Mickey has a sister. Joey has a sister. I want a sister. Sometimes I don't have anyone to play with."

"I know, Sammy. We'll try to have more boys over to play," his mother Emily said softly as she wiped her eyes.

"Go to your mother, son. She's sad that we aren't getting a baby."

Sammy walked to his mother and felt younger by a couple of years. "I want to sit on your 'yap,' Mommy," His lower lip quivered. He took a big breath and tried hard to stop crying.

"'Lap,' Sammy. Try to say your l's," Emily said as she pulled him close to her. "Someday maybe we'll get you a sister."

Sammy turned to his mother and pushed her wavy dark hair back from her face and patted her cheek. Sammy was sure she was the prettiest mother in the whole world with the nicest, kindest, brown eyes. He snuggled against her while she hugged and kissed him.

"Well," Larry said as he walked across the kitchen and hugged them both. "Emily, we'll keep on the list at the adoption agency. Maybe there'll be another baby soon." He stood up and rubbed his hands. "Come on, gang, let's eat lunch."

Sammy slid from Emily's lap and went to sit in the chair at the kitchen table between his parents. He straightened the light green place mat as he lifted his glass of milk and took a sip.

"Ain't I gonna get any presents for my 'bertday'?"

"Birthday, Sammy. Try to say 'birthday' instead of 'bertday.' Say 'aren't' instead of 'ain't,' too." Emily and Larry sipped coffee as they ate their sandwiches.

"Yeah, sure, Mommy." Sammy drank some milk then wiped his mouth on the sleeve of his red knit shirt.

Larry chuckled. "Hard to believe, Sammy, that you'll soon be six years old! You'll have birthday presents! I promise!"

"How many days 'til my bertday?" Sammy picked up his cheese sandwich and took a big bite then had another sip of milk. When he set the glass down, it tipped and he spilled some. He carefully wiped it up with a paper napkin and then watched his father.

Tall Larry crossed to Emily's kitchen desk and tore off a portion of a note pad and returned to the table. Sammy leaned over watching as his father made lines across the paper with the small green pencil he used for his golf score. He marked a letter for each day of the week and made vertical lines under the letters.

"Sammy, this is a graph. Each morning you make an 'X' for that day. See under today, 'S' for Saturday, you draw an 'X.' Tomorrow you make another 'X' under the second 'S' for Sunday. For Monday the letter is 'M.' Every day make an 'X' and when you make one for next Saturday, it will be your birthday!" He handed the graph and pencil to Sammy.

Sammy looked up at his father and smiled then drew the 'X' for Saturday. He shoved the paper and pencil deep in his jeans pocket. After the family finished eating, Sammy jumped up and hopped around the kitchen. "You promise I'll have 'yots' of presents?"

"Not lots," Emily laughed," but you'll have presents."

7

"What presents will I have? I just wanted a sister but not one like Perfect Prissy Sibyl."

"Your cousin's name is Sibyl. Why do you call her Perfect Prissy?" his mother asked as she carried plates and glasses to the sink.

"Aunt Bertha is always calling her Perfect Sissy. So I just call her Perfect Prissy. Anybody that makes her bed and cleans her room every morning before school without being told…" Sammy shook his head from side to side as though he could hardly believe that. It sounded as impossible to him as having nothing to eat except chocolates every meal!

"Try to remember to call her Sybil, son." Sammy was glad to see his mother give a little laugh as she walked over and gently smoothed down her son's cowlick. It sprang back up. "You won't get a sister, but you'll like your presents. Just wait and see!"

—

Chapter Two - Saturday Afternoon

After lunch his father spread the sports page of the Flint Journal out on the table to read it. After his mother stacked the dishwasher, she placed a bouquet of flowers on the table. Sammy reached out and gently touched the petals. They were as soft as his last Beanie baby. "Where did these flowers come from?" he asked.

"Your father bought those pretty red and yellow roses for me because we were told yesterday that we might not get to bring the baby home. Today we know for sure that we won't when your father had that telephone call."

Sammy shrugged his shoulders and had the last word. "Seems to me Daddy would get you flowers when you get my sister, and not when you don't." Sammy tugged at his shirttail and pulled it near a red rose. I 'yike' the red ones best 'cause they match my shirt."

"'Like, darling, not 'yike.' I like the red ones best, too, Sammy. You look handsome in that red shirt!" Emily chuckled.

He hopped over to the window where he noticed an orange moving van. "What does that spell, Daddy? M-o-v-i-n-g."

"'Moving,' son. General Motors is transferring Mr. Taylor from the General Motors plant here in Flint to Kansas City, Missouri."

"His truck isn't paid for," Sammy said hopping back to the table.

"Why are you saying that?" Larry asked.

"You said, Daddy, that if all the cars that ain't paid for were painted orange, it would be a brighter world."

Larry threw back his head and laughed. "I did say that, didn't I?"

Later as the family returned from grocery shopping, Sammy saw black smoke ahead. "It's a fire, Daddy," he said excitedly. "Yet's stop and see it. Yet's stop and see it." Sammy bounced up and down in the back seat as much as his seat belt would allow.

"We might as well," Larry said. "Traffic is blocked anyway."

Sammy trotted up the block ahead of his parents until he was across the street from the burning house. He looked up at the swirling smoke and was fascinated by the curling flames looking as though they were tap-dancing as they tried to break free of the burning roof. Sammy put his hands over his eyes and peeked through his fingers.

He looked again and saw flames whirling and leaping out windows. Sparks and little tufts of smoke fought for space around the door frame.

He heard his mother gasp and his father grabbed Sammy's hand as they saw a young girl run through the crowd and dart into the burning house. A fireman dashed after her.

Sammy looked around and the people watching had scared faces with open mouths and wide eyes. He held tight to his father's hand and leaned close to his wide-eyed mother who had her hand over her mouth.

Suddenly the fireman pushed the girl outside the house so hard she almost fell. Just as he followed her, the ceiling inside fell with a great noise and lots of flickering flames and smoke. Sammy let out a big sigh and felt lots better now that the fireman and girl were safe. She held up a small object. Near the street, the fireman knelt and talked with her.

Soon she started across the street toward Sammy. He saw that she was wearing a torn, dark green sweatshirt with matching pants and carried an old brown backpack. She looked right at Sammy, then stopped and smiled at him. He did not return her smile, as she moved away. He watched her run down the sidewalk.

People began talking and wondering about the little girl. The firemen moved fire hoses. One yelled. It was noisy and confusing.

11

Soot fell on Sammy's hand and red knit shirt. When he tried to rub the soot off his shirt, it left a dirty, black spot. He could feel the heat of the fire. It was noisy and scary. Tugging at his father's hand, he asked, "I wanta go home. Can we go now?"

At home, licking an ice cream cone to get the smoke taste out of his mouth, Sammy asked, "Was it that girl's house that burned?"

Emily, peeling potatoes at the sink, reached into a lower cabinet for a pan as she said, "I don't know. It might have been where the girl lived."

"Where will that girl sleep tonight, Mommy? Did her bed burn?"

"I don't know where she'll sleep, Sammy. I hope she has a good bed someplace but I don't know where. Maybe you should say a prayer for her."

Later in his pajamas made of material printed with baseballs, he asked God to bless his mother, father, grandparents, and to please bring him a sister. Then he whispered, "Make sure that girl has a bed to sleep in tonight."

After his mother kissed him goodnight, he snuggled under his blanket and thought about the girl. As she ran down the street, he noticed her dark green sweatshirt had a hole in the elbow. Her long, wavy light brown hair was pulled back and tied with a dirty looking, yellow ribbon.

He remembered how she looked at him and smiled. He wished he had smiled at her because she looked sad. Where was the house that she was living in now? Sammy snuggled deeper. Was that girl safe in bed someplace?

Sammy had no way of knowing that he would soon be away from his home and bed and having the scariest time of his whole life.

—

Chapter Three - Sunday Morning

The squeaky bark of the neighbor's puppy woke Sammy Sunday morning. That puppy sounds as though it needs Daddy to oil it like he does his lawnmower, Sammy thought as he snuggled deeper under his blanket and blue comforter decorated with a large, yellow Tweety Bird. He lay there a moment studying the Sesame Street characters on his walls. Then he wiggled out and climbed on his bed.

"I'm not s'posed to jump on it," naughty Sammy whispered. But he liked to jump on the bed! He liked the feel of being in the air! He liked to feel his hair staying up on his way down. Jumping up and down three times, he turned around and jumped up and down three more times.

Leaving the rumpled bed, he hopped off, and skipped into the bathroom. Picking up a bottle of the Vanilla perfume his mother used, Sammy looked it over before putting it back. Running down the stairway, he called, "Hi, Emily. Hi 'Yarry.'"

"What's wrong with calling us Mommy and Daddy?" Larry asked.

"Say your "l's," Sammy," his mother said, as the small boy went to her for a hug. "My Norman Rockwell boy," she pulled him onto her lap and smoothed down his Halloween orange rooster tail that sprang up at the back of his head. It sprang up again.

"Norma...who? Why do you say that?" he asked.

"Norman Rockwell was an artist who drew pictures of people. Sometimes the boys in his pictures had red hair and freckles like yours."

"Awwww," Sammy scooted off her lap and rubbed his cheeks.

Sitting next to his father, he said, "Daddy, I'm writing the 'X' for Sunday." He pulled the paper and pencil out of his jeans pocket, put it on the table and carefully marked it.

"That's good, Sammy," his father said and barely looked up as he read an article about Michigan State University's football team, the Spartans, in the Sports section of the Flint Journal.

Sammy hung over his shoulder and saw a picture of the quarterback. "Are you gonna take me to a game, Daddy?"

"We'll see," Larry answered. "I'm not sure we can go when MSU has its first home game this season."

"I wanta go see them win," Sammy said.

15

"So do I, son," Larry smiled at him. "So do I!"

When Sammy heard the telephone ring, he watched his mother hurry to answer it. After a brief talk, she hung up and said, "Mom wants me to come over this afternoon while Dad golfs and help her address invitations for Dad's surprise birthday party."

"His birthday isn't for a month and a half," Larry answered.

"Yes, but you know Mom. She always likes to get everything done well ahead of time."

"Fine with me. You know Gene asked me over to his house to watch the Buick Open Golf Tournament this afternoon. See how my favorite Fred Couples is playing.

Emily set a plate of pancakes in front of Sammy and poured syrup over them. "When you finish your breakfast, get dressed for church."

At church Sammy tried to stop wiggling and peeked out at people between his fingers during prayers. When he saw a man looking at him, he giggled until his father tightly grabbed his shoulder.

Later after a fried chicken dinner at the Olive Garden Restaurant on Miller Road, the family came home again to change clothes for the afternoon. Sammy pulled on a green knit shirt and jeans.

"It's a little cool for July. Should Sammy wear his jacket?" Larry asked.

"Yes. I'm going to wear my beige sweater," Emily answered.

"Let's drive separate cars, Emily," his father said. "You can go directly to your mother's, and I'll go on over to Gene's."

"OK," his mother answered as she pulled on her sweater.

"Why are we going to the store? Are you gonna buy me more 'bertday' presents?" Sammy pulled on his blue, lightweight jacket.

"No, Sammy. We have your presents," she smiled at him. "Golf shirts are on sale at Penney's and your father needs new ones. Also we'll go to the big store because I want to look for a gift for Granddad. Maybe we'll get a sweater or sweat shirt for you to wear to school."

"I'll be in first grade," Sammy bragged. "And I can all ready read. A 'yittle.'"

After shopping Emily and Larry both carried plastic bags. Sammy skipped ahead of them as they walked toward the department store exit.

He spotted a green pup tent over in the sports department. "Mommy, I wanta play in that tent."

"No, Sammy. We need to leave so we can go to Grandma's."

"Am I going?" Sammy tugged at her hand.

"Do you want to go?"

"No." Sammy lowered his head and rubbed one tennis shoe against the other. Sibyl might be there. "I wanta play in that tent."

"Your mother said 'no,' Sammy. You can play in it another time."

Sammy knew when his father used that tone of voice there was no arguing with him. He dragged behind them while they stopped and looked for Larry's favorite shaving lotion.

Sammy gazed longingly at the green tent. He wanted so badly to play in it. He was still mad at his parents for not getting him a sister for his birthday. He'd show them! Grabbing his father's hand he tugged him away from his mother. "Daddy, I'm going with Mommy over to Grandma's," he said.

"All right," his father said absent mindedly as he looked at a display of sport coats. "Be a good boy and stay out of the pasture."

"I will, Daddy," Sammy promised.

He ran back to Emily. "Mama, I'm going with Daddy."

"You are?" Emily asked surprised. "Will you be quiet while they watch golf?"

"I will, Mama. I'll watch Tiger. I like him."

"Larry, Sammy wants to go with you to Gene's house."

Sammy knew Larry was listening to a sales clerk who was holding up a tan sport coat and didn't hear Emily.

Shaking his head at the sales man, Larry turned to his mother. "See you two later, Emily," he said.

A man was talking loudly near her and she didn't hear all of what Larry said.

"OK." She answered pushed the strap of her purse higher on her shoulder. "I'll be at Mom's quite a while."

"And I'll be at Gene's until the Buick Open is over," Larry smiled.

"Be a good boy, Sammy. Hold Daddy's hand in the parking lot," Emily said as she smoothed Sammy's bright hair.

"Yeah," he promised. He skipped away from her, waved, and trotted toward his father as Larry neared the exit door to the parking lot.

So they wouldn't get him a sister for his birthday! He'd make them wish they had! And he was angry because they would not let him play in the tent. He looked at Emily leaving the store on the mall side and his father going out the exit door to the parking lot. He looked at the little tent again. Should he really stay at the store while his parents left? He pursed his lips and thought. Yes, he would!

—

Chapter 4 - Sunday Afternoon

Sammy watched his mother leave by the door going to the mall and saw his father go out the exit door to the parking lot. He dashed across the store and crawled inside the green tent.

Sammy saw poles at each end that held it up. "Cool," he murmured. He smiled as he found a little flashlight that he turned off and on. Shining the light on the tops and sides of the tent and all around again, he whispered. "I like this tent. I want one like it."

After playing in it for a while, he decided, "Better go find Daddy." He stumbled over the sleeping bag as he scrambled out of the tent.

Sammy ran to the door of the store and into the parking lot, but his father was not in sight. The blue Buick was not where his father parked it. Walking around the parking lot, Sammy could not find his mother either. "Well, Clinker Dab!" he muttered. "They're gone!"

Back in the store he walked through the aisles looking for them. "Mama and Daddy will find me," he whispered. Not looking where he was going, he ran into a candy counter and knocked several Hershey candy bars on the floor. He stepped on one. Carefully stacking the

21

candy bars back on the counter, he looked around, then slid the one he stepped on into his pocket. After all the paper was torn and it looked smashed, he told himself. And he loved chocolate!

Looking for his parents again, Sammy wandered down the aisles. "Mama. Daddy," he called several times. He knew they left, but he hoped they had come back. Some customers and clerks looked at him anxiously. An older woman asked, "May I help you find your parents, son?" He darted away because his parents told him not to talk to strangers.

He took the candy bar from his pocket and looked it over. Suddenly he saw a security guard coming his way. "He'll get me for stealing. He'll put me in jail!" he said aloud. Perfect Prissy Sibyl had told him a lot of times that she was going to see that he got put in jail. Shoving the candy bar in his pocket, he ran. Oh, no! A security guard was coming toward him from another direction. His mouth dropped open and he stopped.

Looking toward one security guard and then the other, he saw they were getting closer. "They're gonna get me," he whispered then darted behind a perfume counter and crouched on the floor. On a lower shelf he saw a bottle of Vanilla perfume like the one his mother had. He picked it up to look at it.

Just then the young, blonde clerk stepped backward a few steps, stumbled over Sammy, and fell. She screamed.

Sammy wiggled away from her and scurried to the other side of the U-shaped counter. Another clerk ran to help the blonde clerk. As Sammy peeked around the corner, the blonde got to her feet. Sammy was glad she wasn't hurt.

"I fell backward over a little kid. Where'd he go?" The clerk looked around and the two clerks started over where Sammy was.

His feet flew as he darted out from behind the counter and fled down the aisle. Suddenly he realized he was still holding the bottle of Vanilla perfume. His mouth flew open. He had stolen again. He shoved it into his jeans pocket. When he got home, he would have his mother pay the store for the candy bar and perfume. He knew it was wrong to steal. One of the Ten Commandments he learned at Sunday School was, "Thou shall not steal."

"He's over there," Sammy heard the clerk shout.

Seeing the security guard walking rapidly toward him, Sammy veered off into women's clothing and rushed behind a rack of dresses.

He darted in and out between the racks and nearly ran into a clerk and a customer who were as startled as he was. He changed directions and flew over to a fur coat rack, pulled the coats aside, and stepped in between the bulky garments just as a security guard hurried past in a nearby aisle.

Pulling a fur coat around him, Sammy stuck one arm in a sleeve and was careful to cover his orange hair with the collar. His jeans and tennis shoes showed beneath the coat, but the rest of him was hidden. Almost afraid to breath, Sammy stayed as still as he could for several minutes. After a while he peeked out, with his eyes wide and scared. Seeing two security guards walk up the aisle, he again snuggled deep in the warm, fuzzy coat.

"If there was a lost child running around, he must have found his parents because there's no sign of him now," one security guard said.

Sammy mimicked softly, "If there was a lost child, there's no sign of him now!" He pulled the corners of his mouth down in a little smirk. "I'm pretty smart," he told himself. He stayed where he was but peeked out now and then.

A few minutes later two girls walked over and the overweight girl started looking through the furs. She touched Sammy's shoulder. He slowly moved his arm in the bulky fur sleeve and softly poked the girl in the stomach.

The girl yelled, "Ohhh!" She quickly backed away.

Sammy peeked out but she did not see him. He saw that her mouth was a round "O" and her eyes were so wide the white around the iris showed.

"Hoidy Hoidy," she said. "Somethin's in them furs that ain't supposed ta be there. I'm gettin' out of here."

Sammy watched as the two girls, both appearing frightened as they glanced back over their shoulders, rapidly waggled away. He giggled. "Hoidy, Hoidy," he mocked her. "Somethin's in them coats that ain't supposed ta be there. I'm gettin' out of here." Sammy held the collar up to his face so others could not hear his giggles.

It was fun to scare people! How could he scare someone else?

—

Chapter Five - Later Sunday Afternoon

After hiding for a few minutes, Sammy peeked around but did not see any security guards. He stepped out of the coat rack and carefully kept away from the aisles as he walked among the dresses and tables of clothing.

"I'll call Mommy," he decided. He boldly walked down an aisle.

A tall man walked in front of him. Sammy tried to walk as he did with a long-legged stride. He giggled. The man turned around. Sammy got an innocent look on his face and ran the other direction.

Outside the entrance to the mall, he found telephones and dialed his parent's telephone number. A recorded message told him he must insert a coin or punch in his credit card number. Sammy's mouth flew open. He bent his head toward his shoulder. He had no coins and knew no credit card number. He dialed his parent's number again and again. The recorded message continued and his call did not go through. He kept trying. He raised his head and tried again. Tears popped out just above his lower eyelids and slid down his speckled butterscotch pudding freckled cheeks. "Clinker Dab!" he muttered. "Clinker Dab!"

Two boys came up. Sammy knew they were older—they must be at least ten years old, he decided.

"What's the matter, little kid?" one taunted. "You stupid? Tryin' to call with no money?"

"Kinda dumb, ain't ya?" the other one who might have been as old as eleven asked. "Your hair on fire?" he grabbed Sammy's arm, and reached out to pull Sammy's hair.

Sammy jerked his arm away and ran. He looked back. The boys were chasing him, and he knew they could run faster. Running back into the department store, he fled into the shoe department. After dashing past customers sitting on seats in a row trying on shoes, he looked back.

The boys stopped but glared at Sammy causing him still to be afraid. When the clerks were talking with customers, he slipped into the back room of the shoe department, dashed around tall shelves of shoes, and sat down on the floor panting.

Soon he felt better and began to mimic the boys. "You stupid? Trying to call with no money?" Calling Sammy stupid made him very angry because that's what Perfect Prissy Sybil called him when their parents were not around.

Standing up he aped the bigger boy's actions by reaching out and pretending he was pulling someone's hair and grabbing an arm. Strutting around, he was not scared now as he pretended he was hitting those bigger boys.

A pretty black girl with big dimples and wearing a short red dress with a ruffle around the hem came around the corner carrying three shoe boxes. "What you are you doing here, little boy?" she asked in a kind voice and with a wide smile. "Are you lost?"

"No, I'm not yost. I'm right here," Sammy told her and dashed back out into the store. He squatted by a table of purses and looked around but didn't see the bigger boys.

A short time later a young man with a bouncy walk went by and soon Sammy was behind him. He tried to bounce on his feet like the young man and giggled as he did so.

When the young man turned down an aisle, Sammy ran back to the tent and crawled inside. Noticing a fluffy sleeping bag, he had fun opening and closing it with the long zippers. He felt the soft lining and grinned as he patted the built in pillow. After a while he unzipped it and wiggled down into it. He was tired and zipped the sleeping bag around him.

Putting the flashlight and the perfume bottle close by, he made sure the graph and pencil were in his pocket and snuggled deeper into the sleeping bag. He settled down to sleep not realizing he would have the most terrifying night of his life.

Later frantic Emily and Larry Hendricks returned and searched the store with the help of several security guards. While Sammy's parents stood nearby, a security guard bent and looked into the tent. He shook his head. Emily bent down and looked into the tent, but the bulk of the sleeping bag hid Sammy's small body, and she didn't see her son.

The image of Sammy tugging his red shirt to match the red rose flashed before Emily's eyes. Her little boy looked so sweet in that red shirt.

Holding hands, Emily and Larry walked sadly away. Would they ever find their boy again?

——

Chapter Six - Early Monday morning

"What's that funny noise?" Sammy said aloud. He sat up with eyes wide and an open mouth. He listened but did not hear the noise again. For a moment he forgot where he was and looked around cautiously. He was not in his bed at home. Touching the green tent in the dim light, he remembered that he was all alone in the big department store. With a little shiver of fear he whispered, "I don't wanta be by myself. I'm scared."

He lay back down and covered his eyes with his arm and tried not to cry. Finally he gave a big sigh, gritted his teeth, stuck out his chin and muttered, "I won't cry! I won't cry!" He opened his eyes and sat up again.

Slowly he reached for the flashlight, turned it on, and looked around again. Stretching, he took a couple of big, deep breaths, then crawled out of the warm sleeping bag. Carefully moving the flap of the tent, he peeked out. "It's too quiet," he mouthed the words looking from right to left. "I wish I had Mommy and Daddy with me." He turned off the flashlight.

All he heard was an electric motor hum and distant sound of traffic.

He realized it was the middle of the night, and he was in a strange place. He wanted to be home! He hunched his shoulders and longed for his soft bed. More than anything he wanted to be huddled under his blanket and blue comforter with the yellow Tweety Bird.

"Mommy! Daddy! Mommy! Daddy!" he called and his voice echoed in the near silence. Waiting a while for an answer that did not come, he sadly crawled back into a corner of the tent, sat up, and stretched his arms straight out between his legs, and hunched his shoulders. He tried to keep from crying, but tears rolled down his freckled cheeks.

"This is an awful place for a yittle boy to be," he sputtered again wishing his mother were there to tell him to say his 'l's.' "I'm not even six years old yet." The tent was too small and had no toys! He sniffed as he thought how comforting his mother's arms were when she hugged him. He wanted to be home! His head hung so low that his chin rested on his chest. The tears rolled and he wiped his cheeks and nose with his jacket sleeves.

In a little while he gave another big sigh and whispered, "I'm big! Nothin' scares me." He said it two more times with his voice quavering a little. "I'm a big boy. Nothin' scares me!" Picking up the flashlight he turned it on and looked at everything in the tent again. If he had one like it at home, he would want his mommy and daddy close by.

Rubbing his growling stomach, he remembered the smashed candy bar. The Hershey bar had bits of little boy pocket fluff on it where the paper was torn, but he didn't care. He quickly tore off the paper and took a big bite. Smiling, he decided that Hershey chocolate bar was the best food he ever ate. Smacking his lips, he ate the entire candy bar quickly and licked the paper for the last bite. Crumbling the paper, he tucked it under the sleeping bag.

Feeling better, he pulled his graph and pencil out of his pocket, and made a mark under the 'M' for Monday. Counting the spaces, he said quietly, "Only five more days till my bertday." After a few minutes with a stronger voice he said loudly. "Saturday will be my bertday. I'll be six years old." His voice got louder. "I'm a BIG BOY! And I want a sister! But not like Perfect Prissy Sibyl!" He stuffed the graph and pencil deep in his pocket and turned off the flashlight but held it close.

Peeking out of the tent again, in the store's dim light he could see a row of hanging golf clubs that seemed to be moving toward him. He watched them for a while and decided they were attached to a wall rack. Inching carefully he crawled out of the tent. Because of few dim lights, it was hard to see, but he did not turn on the flashlight. Suddenly he heard a strange thump. His heart pounded and he froze still like a statue.

Shadows made it appear to be a haunted house like the one his parents took him to visit on Halloween. "Are there ghosts and goblins?" he wondered lying on his side on the floor and pulled his arms close and tight and stretched them as far as he could around him. He listened and listened and all he could hear was the dull roar of a motor and traffic outside.

"Mommy. Daddy," he softly called, then got braver and called louder even though he knew he would have no answer.

"I gotta go to the bathroom," he muttered. He stretched his arms forward then started crawling down the aisle. Carefully he stood up and inched forward staying far to the right. He knew the bathroom was just around the corner, as he had been there with his daddy.

Something touched his neck and back of his jacket! He squealed and fell forward. He rolled his eyes from side to side trying to see what was there. Pulling his legs under, he made himself as small as he could. He felt like a huge, hairy, black monster was right behind him and ready to grab him by the back of his neck. He could feel the claws coming closer and closer to his neck. He wanted to scream and yell and even for once wished Perfect Prissy Sybil were near by.

Quietly and carefully he tugged his jacket up high on his head. His heart was pounding and he tried to quiet his fast breathing. Huddling on the floor, he waited and waited. Nothing happened. Feeling braver, he turned on the flashlight and waited some more. Then he pointed it behind him.

Turning it further up, he saw a tennis racket. It was hanging from a rack with other tennis rackets that had swung a little and brushed him.

Wow! It wasn't a monster waiting to grab him after all! "Well, Clinker Dab!" he said aloud and gave a ragged giggle. If Perfect Prissy Sylvia had seen him so scared, she would have called him a dumb, stupid kid again. Good that she wasn't there. Sammy nodded. If she had been, he knew she would have been scared, too!

Standing up, he bravely walked to the bathroom. On the way back he took two long drinks at the drinking fountain. He wasn't scared. Not anymore! He would walk on back to the tent.

Thud. It was a noise close to him. Thud! There it was again! He fell to the floor and again tried to be as small as possible. This time he believed the huge, black monster was three times as big as his father's wheelbarrow. It must be right over him and ready to grab him by the neck.

Now he could almost feel the claws slowly, slowly, getting ready to grab him! Carefully pulling his jacket up over the back of his neck, he crouched close to the floor that he wished would open so he could hide in it. His heart pounded and his eyes were wide open. His hair felt like it was standing on end. He was so scared he thought he was going to die and closed his eyes. Trying to breathe as quietly as he could, he crouched on the floor for a long time.

Again and again he could almost feel the huge monster claws ready to grab him. Without making a sound, he slowly reached a hand around to protect his neck. He moaned a little although he did not mean to do so. He held his breath for a moment hoping the monster did not hear him. He waited quietly. Just as he was about to inch on toward the tent, he heard the strange, soft thud again. It didn't sound as though it was above him this time, but over to the side. He waited and waited and finally got the courage to turn on his flashlight. When he didn't hear any more thuds for a long time, he turned the flashlight toward the sound.

It was a bin of basketballs. Some of the balls moved as they settled. "Clinker Dab! It's only an old basketball," he whispered. Carefully and slowly rolling to his side he looked around and shone the flashlight above him, and there was no black, big as a wheelbarrow monster ready to grab his neck. Well! Good! He was safe!

Sammy let out a long breath of relief with a ragged sigh, hurried to the tent, and snuggled back into the cozy, sleeping bag. "I'm not scared now, but I want Mommy and Daddy," he said softly. "It's awful to be alone." Wiggling around, he reached for the Vanilla perfume bottle, opened it, and sprinkled the wonderful smelling scent over his jacket sleeves then carefully put the lid back on the bottle.

Putting his arm across his face he knew his jacket sleeves smelled like his mother. Maybe he could pretend she was there with him. Rolling over a little, he nestled further down in the sleeping bag and turned off the flashlight. Would he ever get home again? Would he have to live in the store forever? Would he see his parents again? He'd even like to see that ole Perfect Prissy Sibyl.

At Sammy's home, Emily could not sleep. Their bed, usually so comfortable, seemed bumpy and hard. "Where are you, Sammy?" she whispered in the darkness. "I want you home safe in your bed. I miss you so much." Moving carefully, so she wouldn't wake Larry, who she knew was also having trouble sleeping, she slid out of bed and went to Sammy's room. Rummaging around in his clothes hamper, she found the red knit shirt he wore Saturday.

Slowly getting back into bed, she held Sammy's little red shirt close to her face. It smelled of smoke and sweat, and yet there was a sweet Sammy smell, too. Cuddling it next to her on the pillow, the shirt smell soothed her. "God, please bring Sammy home." She felt comforted and a little assured that she would have her precious Sammy home again. Clutching the red shirt, she slept.

—

37

Reva Jo Gordon

Chapter Seven - Monday Morning

The sound of two clerks talking as they walked down the aisle awakened Sammy. He peeked out and the store was now brightly lit. Putting the flashlight and perfume bottle in his pocket, he checked carefully to make sure he had the graph and pencil. With the lights on and daylight coming in from the doors, it was no problem to walk to the bathroom where he washed his hands and face. His face still looked a little scared when he looked in the mirror. He tried to smooth back his bright hair, but it still hung over his forehead. Although he tried to push it down, the rooster tail in the back kept coming back up like a yo-yo on a string.

Walking carefully between tables of merchandise and racks of clothing, he went out the door into the parking lot. "I'm going home to Mommy and Daddy," he said aloud and skipped a little. "They'll be glad to see me." Going down the sidewalk, he skipped some more.

Suddenly the girl from the burning house was before him. She was still wearing the worn green sweat suit. Her hair was now smoothly held back with the worn yellow ribbon. The worn straps of the old backpack held it firmly in place.

"Hi," he said. They both stood there staring at each other. Sammy rubbed one tennis shoe over the other. Finally she asked, "What's your name?"

"Sammy Hendricks. What's yours?"

"Etta Jean," she said as she gave him a big smile.

"Etta Jean," he repeated. "That's a funny name."

"I was named for both my grandmas and I like my name," she frowned and put her hands on her hips. She acted like she might hit him.

Sammy backed away."OK. It's a nice name. I didn't mean anything."

Suddenly it was as though a bubble of giggles started in her stomach and she gave a low, pleasing chuckle. "Hi, Sammy," she smiled.

"Hi." When she smiled Sammy noticed her big, pretty, light brown eyes. Bangs covered her forehead. Her eyes looked sad. Watching her for a moment, he said, "Well, I gotta go. Bye." He turned and walked on. After about six steps, he stopped and turned around.

Etta Jean had not moved and was looking sadly at him. Then she smiled, gave a little wave, turned, and walked away.

I wish I had asked her if it was her house that burned and where she was living now, he thought. I wonder where she's going? Is she going to her home? Sammy worried about her as he walked on.

Suddenly he saw two policemen get out of their car and walk toward him. "They'll get me for stealing the flashlight and perfume. I got to run." Seeing a man and woman walking toward their car, he ran and walked closely behind them. He held his head high and did not look at the policemen.

When the couple reached their car, Sammy ducked behind and around cars and hid until he saw the police car leave. Going back toward the mall, he followed a man dressed in a suit and wearing highly polished shoes. The man kept speaking and smiling to others, so Sammy pretended to do the same.

When the man entered the mall, Sammy turned his attention to a lady wearing high-heeled red shoes. He lifted his heels and twisted at his waist trying to walk like she did. When the woman turned, saw him, and gave him a glare, he scampered off.

He walked in the other direction behind two young women walking and talking as they looked at each other.

"Yes. My boyfriend is so kind," the blond girl said turning to the other.

"Well, my boyfriend wants to take me to Vegas later this month," the dark-haired girl with the ponytail replied, lifting her chin as she turned to the other. "We might get married there."

Sammy turned his head from side to side and mouthed their words with his chin high as he followed them and listened to them brag.

Tiring of the girls, he scampered on down the sidewalk and spotted an older teenager with the bill of his dirty Detroit Tiger's baseball team cap turned to the back. He was carrying out a bouquet of red and yellow roses that he put in the opened back door of a white van.

"He's taking some more flowers that are just like the others to my mommy," Sammy said and smiled. He ran toward the van.

When the teenager went back into the florist shop, Sammy rushed across the sidewalk. Climbing inside the big white van, he pulled back a large green plant in a big pot and managed to squeeze between it and the driver's seat. Lots of flowers were in the van including the bouquet of red and yellow roses.

The driver came out with two pots of flowers and put them inside without seeing Sammy. He slammed the van's back door. Walking to the vehicle, he got into the driver's seat and drove down the street.

"I'm going home," Sammy whispered. He rolled his eyes and laughed quietly as he huddled in his corner.

Taking off his soiled cap, the driver placed it on the seat with the bill turned toward the back. He turned the radio to some blaring rock n' roll music.

With a mischievous grin, Sammy reached up and turned the cap around. The teenager soon looked down. Sammy could see his frown in the rearview mirror. He turned the cap the way he had it.

Putting his hand over his mouth, Sammy tried not to laugh out loud.

When the young driver abruptly turned into a driveway, Sammy had to grab the back of the seat to keep from falling. Peeking out the driver's window he saw the teenager go into McDonald's. Soon he came out carrying a large cheeseburger and a big plastic cup of Pepsi.

Back in the van, the teenager took a bite of the cheeseburger and drink of Pepsi before starting the truck.

The blaring music started again and the driver waved his elbows and shoulders and moved his head in time to the music as he drove.

Sammy rubbed his stomach. That cheeseburger with ketchup showing on one side looked good. He carefully reached up, got the cheeseburger, and took a big bite. Without looking the young man reached for the cheeseburger, and Sammy slid it into the teenager's hand. The driver didn't even notice. Sammy covered his mouth again to quiet his giggles. As they drove along he mimicked the bouncing of the young man's arm and head movements in time to the music.

They stopped at a funeral home. When the teenager went around to open the van's back door, Sammy scrambled between the seats and under the dash on the passenger side. While the young man carried flower arrangements into the funeral home, Sammy ate more cheeseburger and drank more Pepsi. Coming back, the teenager climbed inside the back and rearranged the flowers. He carried one small plant when he again stepped outside and closed the door.

Sammy rushed to hide behind the driver's seat again. The teenager got in the van and placed the plant he carried on the passenger side.

When the young man picked up his cheeseburger, he looked at it with surprise. It was almost gone and so was the Pepsi. He shook his head, frowned, and ate what was left. As he drove he again moved in time to the blaring music and Sammy mimicked him, quietly giggling.

"I'll soon be home," Sammy mouthed the words. "I'll soon be with my mommy and daddy."

An announcement abruptly stopped the music. "Police are searching for a young, red-haired boy, wearing blue jeans, green shirt, and a blue jac...."

The teenager turned to another station.

"That boy's dressed just yike me," Sammy said aloud. He gasped when he realized he had said the words aloud and the driver heard him. The driver turned off the music, and looked around. As he listened and drove, he lifted his chin and sat quietly. Sammy hunched down as much as he could and held his breath.

Soon the driver shrugged and turned up the music. A little later he took off his cap. He stopped the van and took the plant from the passenger side to the house, Sammy turned his cap around and giggled.

The driver wasn't gone long. When he slid into the van, he reached over, picked up his cap, and put it on with the bill toward the front. He took it off and looked at it. "What the heck's goin' on," he muttered. As soon as the music came on, he again moved to it, and seemed to forget his cap that kept turning around.

They kept driving. When the driver stopped and walked to the back of the van, Sammy rushed to hide on the floor by the passenger seat. As soon as the teenager got the flowers and slammed the back door, Sammy dived back behind the driver's seat.

Sammy watched the flowers carefully. The bouquet of red and yellow roses and a few other bouquets were all that was left. Soon the driver pulled into the driveway of a large home, and while Sammy hid, he came around and took the rose bouquet.

Sammy peeked around the seat and saw him pick it up. "Hey," he yelled. "That's not my house. You can't take those flowers to that house!"

The startled teenager's mouth flew open and to Sammy it looked like he jumped a good six inches. Shocked to see Sammy, he nearly dropped the plant.

"Take them to my mommy," Sammy yelled louder.

"Whata, whata you doing in there?" the startled young man said.

"I'm goin' home, and you're takin' those flowers to my mommy," Sammy's yelled.

"I don't know your mommy," the driver mimicked. "These flowers go to this house. You get out of this van. RIGHT NOW! GET OUT!" Putting the flowers on the sidewalk, the driver glared at Sammy.

The teenager suddenly looked mighty big. Sammy opened the door on the passenger side, jumped out, ran down the sidewalk, and hid behind some shrubbery until he saw the van drive away.

"Well, Clinker Dab! Now whata am I gonna do?" he muttered aloud as he stood up and went to the sidewalk. He looked up and down the street both ways. "Where's my house? Which way should I go?"

—

Chapter Eight - Monday Afternoon

"Mommy and Daddy must live around here," he told himself as he walked. He moved with the sun at his back because he knew his parents lived that way from Flint. Before crossing streets, he stopped at and looked each way twice. He waited even if a car was a half block away before he crossed the street just like his mother told him.

Over and over he would look carefully at every house. None of the houses looked like his with the yellow marigolds and pink impatiens in front that he and his mother had set out in the spring. He had also helped his father trim the shrubs. He could certainly tell which was his house when he found it!

On and on he walked. He started counting the houses and when he got to 50, he was discouraged and tired. The sun was now high overhead, and he knew he had walked for a long time.

"I'm so tired," he whispered as he wearily sat down on a curb. "And I'm hungry, too." While resting, he saw a gas station with a little store down the street. Maybe they know where my mommy and daddy live, he thought, and trudged on.

Entering the little store, he asked, "Do you know where Emily and Yarry Hendricks yive?

The girl with greasy looking hair and wearing tight jeans and a denim jacket was taking money at the counter. She shook her head and flirted with a good-looking well-dressed young man.

Sammy stood there waiting and waiting. Finally the customer left. "Please, girl, do you know where Emily and Yarry Hendricks yive? I'm Sammy and I wanta go home." He tipped his head toward his shoulder.

"Yive? Are you so dumb you can't say 'live'? Go away and leave me alone," the girl snarled.

"But I can't find my house," Sammy whimpered.

"So how in the heck do you think I can find it? Now git!"

Sammy left the counter but hid behind a potato chip display watching her. She giggled and smiled at two teenage boys paying for Dr. Pepper sodas, which looked good. Sammy realized he was thirsty. He spotted half a bottle of 7-Up sitting near the coffee machine. He eased up, grabbed it, and drank. It tasted good. He drank more, smacked his lips, and then finished drinking it. He used the bathroom, and walked back out on the streets.

Seeing a bench in a small park, he went over and wearily sat down. It was shady there and felt good to be out of the sun. Tired Sammy stretched out on the bench, put an arm over his eyes, and slept.

When Sammy woke up, he was surprised to see that the sun was far down in the afternoon sky. He used the park bathroom, drank twice from a water fountain, then decided to walk toward the setting sun. Rubbing his growling stomach, he thought surely he would soon find his house and knew his mother would give him something to eat.

After about an hour and a half it was a struggle for Sammy to put one foot ahead of the other. He knew he must if he was going to find his house. He walked and walked and looked at houses until he was too tired to move. Sitting down on a curb he rested for a while. His shoulders slumped and his head rested on his chest. He felt too tired to cry, but some tears seeped out and wet his shirt.

Wearily he pulled himself to his feet and walked on. He walked for a long time when far down the block he saw a orange moving truck.

"They're moving into Taylor's house right by Mommy and Daddy's," he said. Getting energy he didn't know he had, he ran and ran and stopped near the house from which they were carrying furniture.

He watched and waited while they loaded a big blue flowered couch. When they went back into the house, Sammy ran to the driver's side and tried to climb up. He put a knee on the high running board, which had bumps in it. His granddad told him one time that the bumps were to keep the driver from slipping when it rained, but the bumps hurt his knees. He climbed on the step and stood up. He had to swing over to get the door opened and almost fell. Finally he managed to climb inside the high driver's seat. He could hear the men loading more furniture so waited until they walked back into the house before he closed the door.

Looking around he became interested in the dashboard on the truck that looked like it had a lot more dials than his dad's Buick. The worn seats had been blue but were faded now.

Behind the seats was a bunk. "Why, it's yike a bedroom," he smiled. The bunk was long and covered with a brown blanket. A denim jacket was laying on it. Behind the driver's and passenger seats were cabinets that went from the floor to the ceiling. Sammy carefully opened one and saw shirts, jeans, and jackets hanging in the top half.

Drawers were in the lower half and Sammy opened one. "Well, Clinker Dab. Just socks and underwear," he muttered.

He looked around some more. The "bedroom" was painted a dull gray color. It wasn't pretty like his bedroom.

A fairly large cooler was on the floor between the seats and Sammy opened the lid. Good! A nearly full bottle of apple juice was sitting on a plastic bag of ice. Pulling out the apple juice and opening it, Sammy drank directly from the bottle. It was good and cold! He hadn't realized how thirsty he was! Carefully he replaced it on the ice. Then he saw plastic wrapped sandwiches and bananas. He took a sandwich and tore off the plastic. The ham and cheese on white bread looked good. He took a big bite and it was delicious. He took another big bite, then licked the mayonnaise from around his mouth. Soon he ate the whole big sandwich even the crusts of bread and then he ate a banana.

Carefully wrapping the banana peel in plastic wrap from the sandwich, he tucked it down in a corner of the cooler.

Climbing on the bunk, he curled as small as he could as he huddled in the space behind the cabinet on the driver's side. Leaning back and taking a big breath, Sammy folded his hands and closed his eyes. "Please, God, let this truck take me home to my Mommy and Daddy," he prayed.

Sammy heard back doors slam. He lay back on the bunk and quickly covered up with the denim jacket. Soon the doors of the cab opened and a man climbed in from either side. The truck moved away. The men talked but Sammy huddled under the jacket could not hear what they said over the noise of the truck's powerful engine.

After a while the truck stopped and Sammy heard the man on the passenger side say, "Thanks a lot. See you next trip." The man got out and slammed the door.

Sammy pushed the jacket away. He wanted to look out to see if they were close to his house, but the little 'bedroom' had no windows. The truck started again and kept going. Sammy leaned forward. He saw the gray-haired driver, who badly needed a haircut, drive with his arms high on the steering wheel. It looked like they were driving on a highway. When Sammy saw a sign that said "75 and 23" and he knew it was the highway that his parents took to Disney World. Mommy and Daddy don't live this way. "Clinker Dab," he worried.

Leaning back on the bunk, he hoped and hoped the truck would stop at his house. Now it was dark outside. Sammy looked through

53

the windshield at the taillights ahead that looked like rows of red Christmas tree lights. On the other side of the highway, the lights coming toward them looked like a marching army of fireflies.

After a while the whine of the tires that sounded a little like singing and the loud roar of the engine made Sammy drowsy. Lying back on the bunk, he thought of his bed at home again. Snuffing and determined not to cry, Sammy took the perfume bottle from his pocket and sprinkled perfume over both sleeves. Putting the bottle back in his pocket, and checking to make sure he had his flashlight, graph, and pencil, Sammy stretched and sighed. He did not realize the driver was puzzled but pleased about the pleasant smell in his truck. The little boy slept.

When the truck stopped, Sammy woke up and was a little confused about where he was. He could see out the passenger side window and saw a lot of trucks that were stopped. Looking out the windshield he realized they were at a rest stop. He had stopped at this rest stop with his parents on their way to Disney World.

The driver got out and Sammy waited a moment, then jumped out after him, leaving the door closed but not latched, and followed him to the bathroom. He hurried and left before the truck driver. Running back to the semi, he found that it was parked a little on an angle and he couldn't reach the step. He tried to put his right knee on the bumpy step but it was too high. He tried to put his left knee up but still couldn't reach it. "Well, Clinker Dab," he muttered and tried with his right knee again. He had to get into the trunk. It was the only place he knew to go. He grunted and stretched and grunted again, but couldn't get his knee high enough.

Another truck driver came over. "Who you traveling with, Son?"

Sammy looked at him with eyes wide. He stammered. "Uh, uh, my granddad."

"Going to Dayton?"

"Yeah. Sure," Sammy said.

"Well, you're almost there. Have a good time with your granddad." The driver reached up, pulled open the door, and lifted Sammy inside.

"Thanks, Mister," Sammy called just as the man closed the door.

He crawled behind the steering wheel and sat a moment on the passenger seat then spotted a sack of Mars candy bars and a jar of dry roasted peanuts on the floor. He got down to look them over when he heard the driver coming back. He huddled under the dashboard on the passenger's side and froze. He clenched his mouth shut and tried not to breathe. *What if he sees me? What'll I do?*

The driver wearily climbed in, didn't see Sammy, and went back between the seats to the little "bedroom." He threw the denim jacket on the passenger seat. With several grunts, sighs, and bone creaks, Sammy heard him lie down on the bunk. Soon Sammy heard him snoring.

Crawling out from his hiding place, Sammy put a candy bar in each pocket. He managed to open the jar of peanuts and cram some in his mouth. After eating another handful, he ate a Mars bar, then climbed on the passenger seat and pulled the driver's jacket around him like a blanket.

Then he remembered. The man said, "Going to Dayton? You're almost there." Sammy remembered staying at a motel with a pool in Dayton on the way to Florida. He knew he was a long way from home. How was he going to get back to Flint? He stared out the passenger side window and worried whispering, "Now how am I gonna get home?"

Emily sat in the dark of the living room holding Sammy's red shirt. She stared out the window and watched every car that slowly

56

drove down the street. One hand nervously rubbed the fabric of Sammy's red shirt between her thumb and finger. She could just barely make out the yard by the streetlights. So many times she had sat there and watched sturdy Sammy with his Halloween orange colored hair shining in the sunlight as he played on the driveway with his little trucks and cars. How many times had she watched him hurry from the school bus rushing in from kindergarten to pull a paper out of his backpack and proudly show her? The police had been looking for her boy for over 24 hours now. Was he getting enough to eat? Was he warm? She worried about Larry, too, who was having problems eating and sleeping. Taking the red knit shirt from her lap, she held it close to her face.

"Please, God," she whispered, "please bring Sammy home. Wherever he is, please let him be safe. Please let us be a family again."

—

Chapter Nine - Early Tuesday Morning

Sammy woke up as a rough hand with calloused skin stroked his cheek.

"Boy! Boy!" he heard a strange voice calling him. The rough hand continued to stroke his face as Sammy tried to open his eyes.

Sammy kept blinking because of the bright sun.

"Boy! Wake up!"

Finally Sammy could keep his eyes open and looked around the cab of the truck. Again it took him a moment to remember where he was. He turned toward the sound of the voice. The gray-haired driver's gray eyes looked worried. Sammy thought his face had wrinkles like a road map has lines.

"Good. You're awake," the man smiled. "What's your name?"

"My name's Sammy."

"O.K. Sammy, when did you get in my truck?"

Sammy sat straight up. Stretching his arms straight out between his knees, he looked up at the driver with his blue eyes wide. "Oh, Mister, I'm yost. I got yost from my mommy and daddy at the store.

Will you take me home? Please. Please." Sammy's arms, legs, and body were tense. His blue eyes were pleading. "I want to go home awful bad.

"Please take me home." Sammy felt much younger than his almost six years. He bent his head to one side.

The driver's voice was soft and gentle like Sammy's granddad's voice except when Sammy was naughty. "Where do you live, Son?

"I yive at 867 Yager Street. Please take me home. My daddy and mommy want me to come home awful bad. Please, Mister, please." Sammy could not keep the tears back.

"Now, Sammy, don't cry. We'll see what we can do. Sure enough. Forget that 'Mister' stuff and call me Clyde." The truck driver reached under the seat and handed Sammy a tissue. "Just where is this 867 Yager Street?"

Sammy wiped his eyes and blew his nose and handed the tissue back to Clyde who put in a plastic bag that was full of empty paper coffee cups.

"Yager Street. My house has pink and yellow flowers. It's that way," Sammy raised his hand to point but didn't know which way. His hand wavered in the air, and he dropped it.

"All right, Sammy. What town is this Yager Street in?"

"My mommy and daddy and I yive in Flint."

"Flint, Michigan?"

"Yeah, that's it. Flint, Michigan." Sammy's lower lip trembled.

"Well, Sammy, you're a long way from home. Sure, enough. We're close to Dayton, Ohio. You've ridden a long way. When did you get in this rig?"

Sammy gave Clyde a brave smile. "Yesterday I saw you and another man loading this truck with furniture. I thought you were taking it to Taylor's house across the street from ours, Clyde. But you didn't."

"That long, huh?" Clyde scratched his head. "Let me think." Sammy watched him tighten his lips and scratch his neck. "Well, well. Sammy, we'll go to the bathroom and then go get some snacks. We'll figure out a way to get you home."

Sammy washed his face and hands in the bathroom like his mother taught him. At the vending machines Clyde looked for orange juice or milk for him, but didn't find them. He bought Sammy orange soda and four little packets of peanut butter on crackers and black coffee for himself.

Clyde stuck the little packages of crackers into his jacket pocket and carried his big cup of coffee while Sammy carried the orange soda. He put his hand in Clyde's big one. The driver held it firmly as they walked to a picnic table. Clyde put the crackers and his coffee on the table. "Don't sit down yet, Sammy. The benches and table are still wet with dew. The driver pulled a large wad of paper towels from his pocket and wiped the dew off the benches and part of the table.

Sammy looked around at the trees and knew he and his parents had stopped at this same rest stop last year on the way to Disney World.

"Now we can sit down," Clyde said. He opened Sammy's soda, tore open two packets of crackers and handed them to Sammy.

"Ain't you gonna eat?" Sammy asked.

"Yeah. Down the road there's a place that I'll stop and have a big breakfast. Now we gotta figure out how to get you home. Sure enough!"

Sammy drank part of his soda and ate one packet of crackers and started on the other. He drank the soda so fast that he burped big time and he and Clyde both laughed. Sammy pulled his graph and short, green pencil from his pocket. Carefully he marked an X under the T for Tuesday. "Daddy made this graph for me. See it's only four more days till my bertday." He showed the graph to Clyde.

"Well, what do you know? Your birthday, huh? What are you gettin' for your birthday?"

"I wanted a sister, but my mommy and daddy said I'm not getting one," Sammy said wistfully. "Sometimes I don't have anyone to play with. If I had a sister like Joey and Mickey, I'd have someone to play with all the time. Sometimes my cousin—that's Perfect Prissy Sybil—is at my granddad and grandma's house at the same time, but she most always doesn't want to play. She's afraid she'll get d-i-r-t-y." Sammy dragged out word with disgust. "She won't even pick up a worm." Sammy paused a moment then chuckled. "Once I threw a worm on her."

"That was kind of bad of you, wasn't it, Sammy? To throw a worm on a nice girl?"

"Perfect Prissy Sybil is not a nice girl. She tells on me all the time and sometimes she lies. She said I broke my grandma's flower pot and I didn't."

"Do you get punished?"

"Yeah, sure."

"Do you ever do things and not get punished when you should have been scolded?"

Sammy shrugged his shoulders. He looked out toward the trees. Then he looked at Clyde. "Yeah. Sure. Sometimes." He smiled and Clyde smiled, too, and took the boy's small hand. They sat there quiet for a couple of moments. Then Clyde released Sammy's hand, took off his cap and scratched his head.

"Maybe the girl Sybil isn't so bad, Sammy. Sometimes girls don't like to get dirty like boys do. Sure enough. My wife and I have a couple of each and a whole half dozen grandchildren."

"Yeah, well." Sammy looked around. He wanted to talk about something else. "Yast year we went to Disney World and we stopped and ate sandwiches and grapes and drank lemonade. We even had chocolate chip cookies. I yike those best."

"That's great, Son. I have some grandchildren who really like chocolate chip cookies, too. What did you do at Disney World?"

"We had fun except when we were with my uncle and aunt and Perfect Prissy Sybil. That wasn't so good." Sammy paused and took a couple bites of cracker. He looked up at Clyde and smiled. "We had breakfast with Minnie Mouse. She came over and talked to us then she went to the next table and bent over and—and her behind was right next to me. I put my hands toward her behind a couple of times, then I just reached out and pinched her butt with both hands." Sammy giggled.

Clyde chuckled, too. "What did Minnie Mouse do then?"

"She jumped and turned around and laughed. Then she pinched my cheeks. But not hard. It didn't hurt. The bad part was Sybil started in about how awful I was and how she didn't want to go anyplace with me."

Sammy giggled. "Aunt Bertha said I should have my hands slapped, but Mommy just said for me not to do that anymore. She and my dad and Uncle Howard laughed."

Clyde laughed, too. "I bet not many boys who go to Disney World get to pinch Minnie Mouse." He laughed some more and shoved the two unopened crackers toward Sammy.

A police car drove in and parked nearby. Sammy saw Clyde pull his hand back and his fingers start tapping the table. His eyes blinked really fast.

"Sammy, you go over to that building where the vending machines are," Clyde said. "After you see me drive out, go to that

64

police car and tell them you are lost and need to get back to Flint, Michigan. I'd take you over to the police car myself, but, well, I've had a little trouble lately with police. Got it, Sammy? Stay by those vending machines until I get in the truck and leave and then ask the police to help you."

"Will they 'rest me? I stole a candy bar, flashlight, and perfume at the store, and I got two candy bars of yours in my pocket, and I ate your sandwiches and drank apple juice and ate some of your peanuts. My mommy told me it's wrong to steal." Sammy pushed the graph and pencil into his pocket and pulled out the flashlight from his other pocket and showed it to Clyde.

Clyde chuckled. "No, Sammy, they won't arrest you. I heard something on the radio about a boy like you missing. They'll be glad to get you back to your parents. And you can have any food I've got that you want. The police will get you home. I sure wouldn't want any of my grandchildren lost." Clyde stood up, walked around the table and gently tousled Sammy's hair.

Sammy finished his soda pop and crackers then shoved the unopened ones and the flashlight into his pocket. He looked at the police car. "Will they take me home?"

"No, I don't know that they'll take you home, Sammy, but they'll see that you get there. Run over to where the vending machines are. I have to go." Again he tousled Sammy's hair and patted his shoulder then casually started walking to his truck. He stopped and looked back at Sammy then returned, knelt and hugged the small boy. "I sure hope you get home today, Son. I sure hope so. Sure enough!"

Sammy hugged Clyde back then ran to the vending machines and soon Clyde waved to him as the truck lumbered out of the rest stop. "I'll soon be home. I'll soon be with my mommy and daddy!" he said aloud.

He looked at the vending machines and decided if he had money, he would buy candy. Leaving the building, he started toward the police car.

His mouth flew open. No police car! "Clinker Dab!" It must have left when he looked at the vending machines. What should he do now? How was he going to get home? Maybe he wouldn't get home today. His lower lip quavered.

At home Emily struggled to put on make-up. Her face was tense and pale. Sammy disappeared Sunday afternoon and now it was Tuesday morning. Her precious son had been missing so many hours.

"Dear Lord, keep Sammy safe. And bring him home," she prayed her constant prayer. Somehow she knew her plucky little boy was alive. She picked up his little red shirt that was always near her and held it next to her face for a moment. Carefully folding his little shirt, she put it in her purse.

The telephone rang and Emily hesitated before answering it.

"Dear Lord, let it be that Sammy's all right," she prayed. She was afraid to pick up the telephone. "Please don't let it be bad news." Finally she quietly answered.

It was Larry calling from his insurance office. "Honey, Lieutenant Sloan just telephoned and wanted me to let you know. He said a young man delivering flowers Monday morning found a small boy like Sammy hiding in his van. He just told his boss this morning who telephoned police. This young driver described him and I'm sure it was Sammy. Guess he told the driver to take him home."

"Thank God he's safe. How I wish the driver had brought him home!" Emily's voice quavered.

"Don't we! But Honey, we know he's all right and trying to get here."

"Please thank Lt. Sloan for me, Larry." As she hung up the telephone she thought, that was yesterday morning. Where are you today, Sammy? Where did you sleep last night? Are you getting enough to eat?

—

Chapter Ten - Tuesday Mid-Morning and Afternoon

Sammy sat down on the floor by the windows in the little building where the vending machines were located. Watching people and wondering who could help him, but too scared to ask, he sat there for a long, long time. Some of the men and women had interesting walks, but he didn't feel like mimicking them. Besides everyone seemed to be in a hurry.

About an hour later everyone had left the building. Sammy looked out the window and saw a large woman carrying a baby and leading a little boy. A skinny girl with uncombed hair, who was a little older than Sammy, dragged along behind them. All looked kind of dirty and very tired. When they came in the building and passed Sammy, he noticed that a seam was ripping in the seat of the woman's tight pants. He put his hand to his mouth to keep from giggling.

Not watching what he was doing, he stuck out his leg, and the scrawny girl tripped over it. Although Sammy pulled his foot right back, and said, "I'm sorry," the girl came toward him.

She quickly hit him on his cheek with the flat of her hand. It hurt! Sammy scrambled to his feet and hit her arm hard. She took her hand back to swat him again, and Sammy ran out of the building.

He looked back. She was running after him. He ran as fast as he could around to the north of the main building where the bathrooms were located. Three evergreen trees were planted in a cluster and he ran into the midst of them. The branches scratched his arms and hands as he wiggled in among them.

"That girl's as mean as Perfect Prissy Sybil," he whispered. Peeking though the branches he saw her come around the building and stand close to one tree looking all around for him. He tried to slow his rapid breathing and still his pounding heart as he eased around the tree. Rolling his mouth around he got up lots of spit and hurled it at her shoes.

"Mom. Mom," the girl yelled and ran back around the main building. "He spit on me. Come help me git him."

Sammy wiggled out from the evergreens, cautiously looked around, but did not see her or her mother. He dashed into the building and ran in the men's bathroom, where he knew the girl would not follow. With his face squinting with pain, he washed his scratched hands and arms. They didn't hurt as much after he washed. Back outside he decided he should get away in case the girl and maybe her mother would find him and hit him again.

Seeing a family walking toward a table near the back of the area, Sammy ran near them. The father was carrying a big picnic basket. Sammy strolled behind them and began to mimic the bigger boy's measured steps by stepping where he stepped. When the family stopped at a picnic table Sammy circled around them and ran on.

He leaned against a tree to catch his breath. Looking between the trees, he could see a small, white house. Running to the back fence, he climbed over, and walked quickly to the house.

A boy, wearing faded plaid shorts and a white shirt that had a button missing, was playing with a little car in a sandbox made of boards nailed together.

"Hi. Wanta a cracker?" Sammy pulled the two peanut butter cracker packets from his pocket.

The boy nodded, took it, and solemnly unwrapped it. The boys said nothing as they ate their crackers.

"My name's Alex," he said. "What's yours?"

"Sammy. I'm yost. I'm a long way from home and I want to go home."

"You're not lost. You're tellin' a story like I sometimes tell my mama. A made-up story. You're jest kiddin.'"

Sammy's mouth flew open and he rolled his eyes. Alex didn't believe him! Sammy stared at him and wondered how to make him believe he was lost. Bending his head to one side, he worried.

Alex, making a noise like an engine, pushed his little red toy car around in the sandbox. He looked up at Sammy. "Wanta play?"

Sammy nodded and picked up a little truck with a wheel off and filled it with sand. The boys made car and truck noises as they drove their car and truck making tracks in the sand. After a while they climbed a tree, and later Alex picked up a softball with a torn covering which the boys tossed back and forth. Sammy was glad that Alex couldn't throw the ball or catch it any better than he could.

At noon Alex's mother came outside. "I didn't know you had a friend playing here, Alex."

"This is Sammy. He told a pretend story that he was lost. Mama, can he have lunch with us?"

"I s'pose he can. Come on in."

Inside the house Sammy looked around at the peeling wallpaper and worn carpeting. This house certainly didn't look pretty like his. "May I use your bathroom?" he asked.

The towel had strings hanging from the hems and the middle was so thin Sammy could almost see through it.

Alex's mother served him a big bowl of vegetable soup with hunks of potatoes and carrots. Sammy liked it although he usually wouldn't eat carrots. He especially liked the piece of warm cornbread spread with margarine that she handed him. The glass of cold milk tasted good, too.

"Where are your parents?" Alex's mother asked as she sat at the table that was covered with a clean pink, plastic cover and ate with the boys.

Sammy looked at Alex and thought she wouldn't believe him anymore than Alex did. "They're over at the rest stop. Our car broke and my dad's fixing it. After while I'll go back there."

The woman nodded. "I know what it's like to have a car break down. I hope your dad can fix it." She smiled at Sammy.

After finishing the soup, Sammy looked around for dessert but there didn't seem to be any. He reached in his bulging pockets and pulled out the two candy bars and gave one to Alex.

Alex's eyes were big. "Thanks, Sammy. Thanks." Before unwrapping it Alex went to a drawer and came back with a paring knife.

"Help me cut it so Daddy and Tommy and you will have some," he said to his mother.

"What you doin'?," Sammy asked.

"We don't get candy bars very often. I want Mama and Daddy and my brother Tommy, who's over at his friend's house, to have some."

"Oh." Sammy thought a moment, then pushed his candy bar over. "Keep mine for them to eat later."

Alex's mother said, "Thank you, Sammy. You're a fine boy." She smiled.

Sammy thought it would be awful not to have candy bars when they wanted one and have to divide it. He peeked into the refrigerator when she put the rest of the soup in it. They didn't have a packed refrigerator like Sammy had at home. He felt bad for them. Alex's mother was really pretty when she smiled, but not as pretty as his mother. Sammy sighed.

Alex and Sammy each ate a portion of the candy bar then went back out to play. Alex showed him some kittens in an old shed. They played with them for a long time.

Alex's brother came home. He was riding an old rusty bicycle. He was curious about Sammy. He asked a lot of questions about his father's car that Sammy couldn't answer. Sammy decided it was time to leave.

"Bye, Alex. Thanks for lunch and playing with me," Sammy said and trudged out of their yard, back through the trees, and climbed over the fence.

What should I do now? he wondered. How can I get home? Maybe I can find somebody to take me. How will I find someone to take me home?

—

75

Chapter Eleven - Tuesday Evening

Sammy leaned against the main building and again watched men, women, teenagers, and children for a long time. He wanted to ask somebody to help him get home, but everyone was in such a hurry. Nobody even looked at him.

He saw a girl that looked like his cousin Sybil and ran toward her. It wasn't Sybil. Just as well, he thought. The last time they were at her parent's house, she tripped him and he fell hurting his hands and knees. "If you tell, I'll say you're lying, and they'll believe me," she sneered.

Later Sammy "accidentally" spilled his grape juice on her pink dress. When she squealed and told her mother, Sammy said, "Oh, I'm sorry. The glass was a yittle wet, and it slid right out of my hand." His father shook his head at Sammy as though he knew Sammy did it on purpose.

It was getting dark when a young, pretty girl with dimples smiled at Sammy as she went into the women's bathroom. When she smiled one front tooth lapped over the other one a little bit. He thought that made her face look interesting. He waited until she came back out of the bathroom then rushed up to her. "Are you going to Flint, Michigan?"

"No, I'm going to Cincinnati to see my boyfriend."

"I got yost from my parents and I have to go home to Flint, Michigan."

She reached up and checked a heart shaped earring. "Nobody at this rest stop is going north. Everyone's going south. You'll have to go to that other rest stop across the highway to find someone going north."

They walked outside and watched the cars, trucks, busses, and motor homes zooming by.

"I'll have to walk across that?" Sammy asked his voice quavering.

"Yes, if you want to go north." Quietly they watched the traffic. Sammy thought the roar sounded really scary.

"I'd be awful scared to walk across that big street," he said pointing to the highway. He bent his head toward his shoulder and worried.

"Tell you what. I'll drive you across," she said smiling at him as she pushed back her dark curly hair and smiled showing her crooked tooth.

"Will you?" Sammy stretching up and grinning at her.

They climbed into her small, tan car, and she helped him fasten his seat belt. "What's your name?"

"I'm Sammy Hendricks and I want to get home because Saturday is my bertday. What's your name?"

I'm Vic. Well, really my name is Victoria Reynolds but everybody calls me 'Vic.' When we get to the other side, I'll go to the vending machine building and see if I can find someone going north to Flint," she told him. "How did you get here anyway?"

"I hid in a truck on the way here. I can hide in a truck going that way," Sammy pointed north. "But I don't want whoever it is to see me. He might not let me go with him."

After reaching the other rest stop, they went to the vending machine area. "OK," Vic whispered. "I'll find out who's going to Flint. You go outside and stand by that wastebasket and wait for me." Sammy left but stood where he could see her. She pretended to put money in the vending machines and acted as though they were not working. She would walk to one then another and listen to the men talking.

Sammy got cold waiting for her and felt hungry and sad. It was really dark, he wasn't home, and a few tears slid down his face. He went to the bathroom. Back outside he pulled out the perfume bottle, sprinkled a little on his jacket sleeve, then pushed the bottle deep into his pocket again. He went to the other side of the wastebasket and leaned against it as he watched her.

The girl smiled at a big, dark-bearded man wearing dirty jeans and a faded gray sweatshirt. He had lots of greasy looking black hair sticking out from under a blue cap.

A shorter, cleaner looking man stood drinking a cup of coffee. "I'm on the way to Chicago. Where are you going?" he asked the bearded man.

"I'm on the way to Flint. S'posed to have the load there by 9:00 o'clock. Reckon I'll have time to stop and spend a few hours with the wife on the way," he winked. "We live near Flint."

Both men started out and the pretty girl stopped the bearded man. "I've always wanted to see the inside of a truck. Will you show it to me?" She smiled, lifted her eyebrows, and pushed back her dark curls.

With her hand behind her trim waist she motioned for Sammy to follow a little way behind them.

"Sure," the bearded man said and strutted a little. "My rig's over this way."

The girl walked with him laughing and talking. When they got to the truck, the man opened the driver's side door.

"Ohhh," the girl squealed. "Please go around and open the other door. I'll peek in here and then come around and climb in on the other side."

The man walked around the truck. The girl kissed the top of Sammy's head, then hurriedly lifted him, and pushed him inside. He stumbled over a cooler, then wiggled as fast as he could back to the bunk.

The truck driver opened the passenger door and turned around to look for Vic. Sammy saw her running back to her car. The bearded man had such a strange look on his face that Sammy put his hands over his face to keep from giggling out loud. He saw the truck driver frown and walk around to the driver's side.

Sammy looked around the sleeping compartment. He sniffed. The truck didn't smell clean. Papers including fast food sandwich wrappers, empty heavy paper soda cups, and dirty clothes lay around. Sammy pushed some to one side, then huddled on the bunk behind the cabinet.

The driver climbed in the truck muttering. "Where'd she go?" Then he said some bad words about the girl. Sammy put his hands over his ears.

The driver pulled on to the highway and Sammy could see the signs along the side of the road. He could read a little and knew the number '75 North' meant they were going toward home. He was really going home! He leaned back and smiled. Soon he would be with his parents again!

The driver acted like he was mad at everyone. He shook his fists at car drivers and sometimes said very bad words. When he did, Sammy would cover his ears and quietly giggle. His daddy would never say words like those! Sometimes the driver would pick up his thermos bottle, hold it between his legs, and pour coffee into the lid and drink.

Sammy mocked him. He mouthed the bad words, but never said them out loud. He would shake his fists when the driver did. The driver said "You..." or "Blast you're..." and worse words. Sammy giggled wondering what his parents would say if he said those words! He would be afraid to try except maybe around Perfect Prissy Sybil!

For a long time he listened and shook his fists like the driver did at other drivers, and mouthed words he had never heard before. Then tiring of the game, he leaned back and rested. Rubbing his stomach he eyed the cooler. Since it was dark in the sleeping place, Sammy didn't think the driver would see him. Carefully with his feet hooked around the sides, he pulled the cooler back. The thermos bottle rolled back, too, and Sammy pushed it forward. Carefully and quietly he pulled the lid off the cooler. Cold fried chicken, Oreo cookies, and a quart of milk were inside.

First Sammy drank from the carton of milk, then ate chicken. He wiped his hands on the dirty blue blanket, then careful not to rattle the paper, pulled out about seven Oreos. He ate four, and shoved three in his pocket. Replacing the carton of milk and the cooler's lid, he carefully pushed it back between the seats.

Getting sleepy, he started to crawl under the blankets but they smelled like sweat. Opening the perfume bottle he poured a lot more than usual on his jacket sleeves.

The driver looked around and sniffed and sniffed. Sammy knew he could smell the perfume and grinned.

The driver went faster and jerked the truck around so that it was hard for Sammy to stay on the bunk. One time he braked so suddenly Sammy hit his head on the cabinet. He rubbed it until it stopped hurting.

Sammy wished the truck driver wouldn't yell so much at the other drivers. He sounded mean. Sammy was so tired and sleepy. It was no fun listening to the driver and watching the lights. Tonight he couldn't even pretend that the lights ahead of them looked liked red Christmas tree lights or those coming looked like marching fireflies. He lay down on the bunk and pulled the smelly blanket up and slept.

Much later after Sammy slept a long time; something hit his leg hard and woke him up. He was startled and afraid. He sat up and rubbed his leg and realized the driver had thrown back a bulky road map on the bunk and hit him with it. That made him really angry.

He remembered something else in the cooler and carefully with his both feet pulled it back again. It was a jar half full of pickles. Carefully and stretching his leg full length he pulled back the thermos bottle. Holding it between his legs like the driver did, he opened it,

83

then opened the jar of pickles and poured pickle juice in the thermos. He put the jar of pickles back in the cooler, replaced the cover, and pushed it forward. With a smirk, he put the lid back on the thermos and rolled it forward.

Nearly a half-hour later while Sammy waited patiently, the driver reached down and picked up the thermos bottle. Sammy watched holding his breath.

Sure enough, the driver held the thermos between his legs, took off the lid, poured some in it, and drank. He spat on the floor.

"BLAST..." the driver yelled, threw the thermos on the floor, then yelled a whole lot of bad words.

Sammy covered his mouth to quiet his laughter. He laughed and laughed.

Later he peeked around the cabinet and watched road signs. When he saw the sign "Flint" he knew he was getting close to home. He smiled and smiled thinking about how happy his mommy and daddy would be to see him.

Suddenly the man took an exit off the expressway. I'll yell at him and tell him to take me home, Sammy thought, then decided that maybe he should be quiet. The man might be mean enough to hit him or make him get out of the truck in the dark.

The driver drove quite a way on a smooth road, then turned onto a bumpy road for a little way. He stopped and got out of the truck. Sammy peeked out and saw him enter a brown house with several trees in front.

Waiting and waiting, Sammy got sleepy. To stay awake he ate the other three cookies. Finally he lay down on the smelly bunk. "Please, God. I didn't get home today. Please help me get home tomorrow. How am I gonna find Mommy and Daddy after I get to Flint? How can I find my house? Please have somebody help me," he prayed.

Chapter Twelve - Wednesday Morning

Sammy knew when the driver came back to the truck and started driving again, but he soon went back to sleep.

He woke up and nearly rolled off the bunk when the driver lurched to a stop at a red traffic light long after daylight. Scrambling to hide behind the cabinet Sammy hit it with his elbow. "Clinker Dab!" he muttered.

The bearded driver heard the noise, looked back, and saw him. "Hey, Brat? Whata you doin' in my truck?"

"I'm yost. I'm trying to get home. Will you take me?"

"NOOOO," the driver yelled. "I won't take you home. You get out of here. I could get in trouble by you bein' in my truck?" Sammy nearly fell off the bunk when the driver jerked to a stop along the curb and hurled out of his seat.

Sammy tried to push the driver's hands away that grabbed the front of his jacket, but the bearded man was too strong. Sammy felt himself yanked to the front seat. He was scared of the driver who now looked awfully big and mean. When the driver jerked open the passenger door, and gave Sammy a shove, he flew out the door and onto the sidewalk.

He landed on his hands and knees. His jeans protected his knees a little, but his hands were skinned and hurt. He looked up at the driver who stared at him out the truck's open door.

"Get outta here, you little punk, or I'll beat the living daylights out of ya."

Sammy got up and ran and ran down the sidewalk. His hands and knees hurt. He ran toward a big building but didn't know where he was. He hoped he was in Flint. Tears filled his eyes so that he was seeing through a blur. Stumbling on down the sidewalk, he failed to look for traffic.

Starting across a street, he was suddenly jerked roughly backward. He fell back hard just as a big bus rambled by so close he felt the heat of the engine and strong smell of the fuel. He twisted around and looked at the person who had so roughly pulled him backwards.

"That hurt," he said.

"So what? Better than you being dead!"

Surprised to see the girl from the burning house and the one he said "Hi" to Monday morning, Sammy thought a moment. "Etta Jean?" he asked.

"Yeah. Don't you ever look where you're goin'?" The girl scrambled to her feet and stood with her hands on her hips. "You would have been hit and killed by that bus if I hadn't pulled you back. What's the matter with you?" she yelled.

Sammy stared at her. He knew he almost stepped in front of the bus. He shivered. He could have been killed. He slowly got to his feet still staring at her. "You hurt me."

Her voice softened. "Don't you know I just saved your life?" She gently brushed dust from his jacket and pulled down a sleeve.

"Yeah. Sure. Thanks." Sammy looked her over. She was maybe three years older than he was. Still dressed in the old green sweatshirt with matching pants, he now saw the cuffs were all ragged and there was a big hole in one knee. She had no jacket. One of her worn out once white but now dirty gray tennis shoes was tied with a dingy string. Her light brown hair looked tangled. It was long and wavy, and she had it tied back with the twisted yellow ribbon. Her bangs were tousled.

She looked at him with concern. "What are you doin' here anyway? Where's your mom? Didn't you say your name was Sammy?"

Sammy nodded. "I'm yost," Sammy said as stretched his fingers trying to take the sting of his skinned palms away. "I want to go home to my mommy and daddy? Is this Flint?"

"Sure it's Flint. Was that your mother and father I saw you with last Saturday? Were they your real mother and father?"

"Of course, they're my real parents!" Sammy was annoyed at her dumb question. "Doesn't everybody have real parents?" Sammy frowned at her and pushed his jacket sleeve up again."

"I don't have parents," Etta Jean said so softly, Sammy barely heard her.

A noise caused Sammy to look about 20 feet away, and he was fascinated to see an old lady pushing a grocery cart filled with objects in brown paper bags. She was dressed in three dresses. Her top dress was green, and then a blue flowered dress showed under that with a gray shiny one showing under the blue one. She was wearing a red yarn cap and straight gray hair stuck out in all directions from under it. She would say, "One, two three," and take a step with each number, then lift the other foot and pause. Then she would count again, take three steps, and then pause with her foot lifted. She kept doing that over and over. He and Etta Jean moved to the grass to give her room on the sidewalk.

"What's the matter with her. She crazy?" Sammy whispered. He started walking behind her just like she did with three steps and a pause then three more steps and a pause, giggling as he did so.

Etta Jean ran up to him and grabbed his arm. "Stop that! Stop mocking her!" she hissed. "It's not nice to make fun of people. Kate's not crazy. Her kids said she had to move from her house, and she ran away from them. Hank and I have been helping her hide from everybody."

"Oh." Sammy felt embarrassed that Etta Jean scolded him. He put his hands in his pocket and stared up at a tall building.

"Come on." Etta Jean ran down the sidewalk and turned into an alley. Sammy hurried to keep up. She crawled into a big cardboard box and Sammy crawled in after her.

"What's this?" Sammy remained on his hands and knees. "What's this box? What was in it?"

"I don't know. See it's big. I can sit up in here and there's lots of room to lie down at night. Hank got it for me. This is where I live."

"You really, really yive here?" Sammy rolled his eyes. He sat across from her. "Was that your house that burned?"

"Yes," Etta Jean admitted looking down and tearing at a long nail.

"Then you didn't have anyplace to yive?" Sammy tapped the thin cardboard 'walls. "Naw, you don't yive here..."

"Yes, I do!" Etta Jean put her hands on her hips again and looked angry as she stared at Sammy. "After my grandma's house burned, our neighbor man, Mr. Lyons, said Mrs. Lyons had to take Grandma Etta to a nursing home because she couldn't take care of herself anymore, and he drove me to my stepfather's. I stayed there 'til Sunday night."

"You were dumb to go in that house when it was on fire."

Etta Jean smiled. "Yeah, I know I was. But I had to get my picture." She spoke in a soft voice.

"I wish I had grabbed my book and some clothes, but I didn't have time, 'cause the fireman came and pushed me out."

"You about got all burned up." Sammy looked all around the cardboard box. He pondered over her what she had told him and looked around. "You got no windows."

"Yeah. So what? I can keep the 'door' flaps open and that gives us light. We can see in here." The girl pulled a small picture from her backpack but when Sammy reached for it, she pulled away and held it close to her under the palm of her hand.

"Why don't you yive with your mommy and daddy?"

"'Cause I don't have any. I told you. Now quit asking questions. You hungry?"

Sammy nodded and rubbed his stomach. "Show me that picture."

Etta Jean smiled as she held out the picture. "It's shows my mother holding me. She was so pretty. Don't I look cute?"

Sammy studied the picture of a young woman holding a plump, smiling baby.

"That baby's you?"

"Sure, it's me. See on the back it says 'Marie and Baby Etta Jean.' I was named Etta for my mother's mother and Jean for my father's mother. I've got both my grandmas' names," she said proudly and carefully took the picture from Sammy and replaced it in her shabby backpack. "I like this better than anything I have. That's why I had to run in the house and get this picture of my mother and me."

"Where's your mother now?"

"She died. She got the big 'C'," Etta Jean whispered as she looked down. "I took care of her when she was sick."

"What's the big 'C'?"

"Cancer," Etta Jean whispered very softly. "It's really, really bad. My mom got so she hurt almost all the time and sometimes she'd cry because she hurt so much. She couldn't eat, and she got all skinny. I was in kindergarten, but I stayed home a lot and took care of her. I'd hug and kiss and helped her wash and get her stuff to eat and drink and help her to the bathroom. Grandma Etta came when my step-dad wasn't there and helped take care of my mom, too. Then they took my mother away to the hospital and I didn't see her anymore. She died. I was five then." She turned away and combed her bangs with her fingers.

"Well, why don't you yive with your daddy?" Sammy squealed as a big, black arm poked into the box flap.

"Hank, Sammy's here. You scared him. He's lost." Etta Jean laughed her deep bubbling, belly laugh.

The man stooped down and looked into the box. "Hi, Sammy," his voice was low and deep. "How did you get lost?" The dark skinned man who smiled had a kind face and Sammy immediately liked him.

"I was in a store with my mommy and daddy and told my mommy I was going with my daddy then I told my daddy I was going with my mommy, then I played in a tent and they yeft." Sammy sniffed loudly. "I'll never do that again!"

"Well, now. That's too bad, fella. I hope you get home. Here's a doughnut for you kids."

Etta Jean took the still warm doughnut. "Thanks, Hank," she said as Hank left.

"Who's was that man?" Sammy asked thinking about how he first scared him.

"That's Hank. He lives in boxes down the street. He has a mother that he stays with sometimes, but he said he'd stay here as long as I am here to help take care of me. He brought me this blanket and brings Kate and me food when he can."

Sammy looked at the old brown and rust colored blanket which was ragged and dirty looking. He hoped Etta Jean didn't see him sniff.

She carefully broke the doughnut in half and gave part of it to Sammy who greedily ate it while Etta Jean ate hers more slowly.

"What about your daddy?" Sammy asked again.

"My father was an important man, my mom said. He hadn't worked too long in being a lawyer when he died. My mom said that was why he didn't leave us money, 'Cause he was just getting started, you know." She put the remaining small piece of doughnut in her mouth and chewed slowly. Then she spoke so low, Sammy could hardly hear her. He watched her turn her hands over and over as though she was washing them. "Someone went through a stop sign and hit my father's car and he died, my mom told me. She said it made her awful sad, but then I was going to be born and she was happy when she got me."

"That sucks." Sammy leaned forward as he listened.

"Don't say that. My grandma said not to say that word," Etta Jean told him.

Sammy turned away for a moment. He felt hurt that she scolded him again, and that he said something he shouldn't. After a few minutes he turned back to her. "Then what happened after your mom died."

"Sammy, I'm tired of your questions." She reached out and gently took Sammy's hand and opened his fingers. "Does your hands hurt? They got some blood on them."

"Yeah, they hurt." Bending his head to one side he sniffed loudly.

"Come on. We better go get them washed." Etta Jean scrambled out of the cardboard box and Sammy straightened his head and crawled after her.

"You're dirty," he told her looking at her green sweat suit.

"I do the best I can." She looked away.

Sammy could tell her he had hurt her feelings. He reached out and touched her sleeve. "I'm dirty, too. It's all right."

Etta Jean turned and smiled.

"You're real pretty when you smile." Sammy thought she really was with her big, brown eyes, turned up pert nose, and full lips. She even had a dimple in her chin much like Sammy's.

"Nobody's ever said such a nice thing to me for such a long time," Etta Jean beamed and took Sammy's hand for a moment.

Sammy skipped and hopped a few steps. He certainly wanted to be home, but it was fun being with Etta Jean.

96

As they walked along he wondered. Did she have any other clothes? Was she cold at night sleeping in the cardboard box? When he got home, he would have his mother buy her some clothes. If he ever got home…

—

Chapter Thirteen - Wednesday Mid-Morning and Afternoon

Sammy followed Etta Jean up some steps into a big office building.

"Now you go in there," she pointed to a 'Men's' sign, and I'll go in the other one. Wash as good as you can. Use soap on your hands to get rid of the germs, my mother used to say. I'll wait out here for you."

After they used the bathrooms, Etta Jean led Sammy three blocks over to the familiar golden arch at McDonald's. She waved at someone as they passed the windows, then motioned for Sammy to sit on a step at the back door.

They waited a while until a pimply-faced teenager pushed open the door and shoved two small hamburgers and two cartons of milk into their hands.

"Now, git, Etta Jean. You know I'm not s'posed to do this."

"I know, Andy. Thank you very much."

Etta Jean and Sammy walked back to the office building where they sat on the steps and drank their milk and ate hamburgers.

"After we go into the bathrooms again and put our trash in the waste basket, we'll go to a park and play."

"Are you gonna help me get home?"

"Later," Etta Jean said. "I gotta think about it. It's nice to have someone to talk to…"

On the way to the park Etta Jean said, "Step on a crack, break your mother's back."

Sammy started to say you don't have a mother, then thought about how lucky he was to have pretty Emily as a mother and didn't say anything. He joined in her game. They hopped and skipped, always careful not to step on cracks, and tried to use every other foot in jumping over the cracks. When they accidentally stepped on a crack, Etta Jean would laugh, deep and bubbling. Sammy liked hearing Etta Jean's deep laugh. When she laughed, he laughed, and the four blocks to the park went fast as the two hopped, skipped, and laughed.

Tall trees made lots of shade in the park. They made their way to a swing set and sat in the big swings, pushing off with their feet and moving their bodies to make the swings go higher.

"I'm going higher," Sammy sang.

"No, you're not. I am," Etta Jean smiled at him.

99

They moved on to climb on play structures and then went to sit on the end of a picnic table where they rested as they swung their legs.

"How long have you been lost?" Etta Jean asked.

"I'll show you my paper." Sammy got the graph and pencil out of his pocket and placed it on the table. He carefully made the X for Wednesday. "Only three more days till my bertday. It's Saturday and I'll be home," he smiled at her. "I wanted a sister," he added wistfully. He put the paper and pencil back in his pocket checking to make sure he still had the little flashlight and perfume.

"When did you get lost?"

"I got yost Sunday after church. I wanted to play in a tent 'cause my parents wouldn't get me a sister for my bertday. I'll be six years old."

"It's 'lost', Sammy. And it's birthday. Talk plain." Etta Jean told him. She smiled at him. "I'm nine years old."

"Oh." This time when she scolded him, Sammy didn't care. They swung their legs more and both were quiet.

After a while Etta Jean asked, "Why do you want a sister?"

"My friends Joey and Mickey have sisters and they're real nice. They always have somebody to play with. Not like my cousin Perfect Prissy Sibyl."

"What a name! Perfect Prissy Sibyl. What do you call her that?"

"Because Aunt Bertha calls her Perfect Sissy. Do you know Sibyl even makes her bed every day before she goes to school? She always gets good grades and never gets dirty, but sometimes she's mean to me."

"What does she do that's mean?"

"Well, one time she put her gum in my hair and it stuck. It hurt when my mother pulled it out. I had just put my gum in the trash barrel, so Sibyl took the gum out of her mouth and smashed it in my hair. Then she told Aunt Bertha, who always, always believes her, that I smashed my own gum in my hair. I told Mommy yater and Mommy said to stay away from Sybil. That she was jealous of me because she was the only grandchild for a yong time, then I came along and get attention from my grandparents. What's jealous?"

"I don't really know except at school sometimes the teacher seems to like the clean kids with nice clothes better than me. When I feel bad about that, I'm being jealous, I guess." Etta Jean explained. She put her arms over her head and stretched.

"That man in that green car that just drove by yooks like a man my dad knows. He talks to him at church sometimes," Sammy said.

Etta Jean took a deep breath. "It's nice that you get to go to church. I barely remember going to church with my mother before she got sick. I was little then. I liked going."

"Where did you yive after your mother died?"

"I went to live with Grandma Etta. My granddad died a long time ago. First I stayed with my stepfather, but he didn't want me. See my mom married my stepfather when I was three. I remember him being really nice to us and bringing me a doll and my mom flowers before they got married. Then after they were married he got mean. He was mad at my mom a lot. She went to work and always gave him her money. If she didn't, he would hit her. When she worked I stayed with my grandmas. They thought I was special." She sighed and was quiet for several minutes. "That was a long time ago."

"You mean your stepfather hit your mother? I didn't know men hit women except once I saw a man hit a girl on TV, but that was just a show."

"Yeah, sometimes. She told me not to tell my grandmas, so I didn't."

"Then what happened," he turned his head and stared thoughtfully at Etta Jean.

"My mom and I had a secret. We were going to move away and not live with my stepfather anymore. Then Mom started feeling bad, so she said we would wait to move until she felt better. But she never felt better so we stayed. He was mean. He tore up the book Grandma Jean got me for Christmas, then took my doll and swung it against the wall until the head broke and the stuff inside fell out."

"He tore up your and book. And broke your doll? Why'd he do that?"

"I don't know."

"Did he hit you?"

"Oh, yeah. Sometimes when I was bad. My stepfather moved us to an awful apartment and wouldn't let anyone come to see us. Grandma Etta came though when she knew he wasn't home. Grandma Jean and Granddad moved a long ways away because General Motors gave my Granddad a better job. They didn't come to see us anymore. I haven't seen them for so long, I forgot what they look like."

103

They were both quiet for a while. "My daddy spanked me for running into the street, and my mom spanked me for biting Dougie. I didn't yike Dougie. I was glad when he moved away."

"I never had kids to play with."

Sammy looked at her. It must have been awful for her to live with someone who was mean. "Mommy and Daddy are real nice to me though," Sammy told her with pride. He swung his legs more. "Did you yike to stay with your grandma?" he asked.

"Yeah. Grandma Etta knew my stepfather didn't want me. Right after my mother died, Grandma Etta came and got my stuff and me. I missed my mother a lot and so did Grandma. She hugged me and kissed me and combed my hair. She cooked good food and got nice clothes for me. I went to school everyday 'cause I'd missed so much kindergarten taking care of my mom. I tried hard at school and there was one girl named Angela who helped me with my reading and numbers."

Etta Jean reached up and combed her bangs with her fingers. "Angela ate lunch with me and we played at recess and noon. I liked school."

"So everything went ok?" Sammy hopped down from the table and made piles of dirt with his tennis shoes.

"No, not everything. I missed my mother, and I missed Grandma Jean and Granddad. But Grandma Etta helped me with my schoolwork, and we played games, and watched TV together. We had fun." Etta Jean scratched her nose. "Grandma made me a dress once. It was real pretty."

"What happened to your dress? What happened with your grandma?"

"I got too big for my dress. I started second grade and not long after school started, I came home and my grandma was lying on the floor. I had a hard time waking her up. Mrs. Lyon, our neighbor lady, took her to the doctor. The doctor said she had a little stroke. Then she had some more little strokes. She started forgetting a lot." Etta Jean paused and took a deep breath.

"Then did your grandma get well?" Sammy leaned his head toward his shoulder.

"No. She started doing weird things. Like one time she put the milk carton in the oven then turned on the oven and it got on fire. She got worse then, and I stayed home sometimes in second grade and took care of her like I did my mother. Sometimes she was like her old self and we had fun."

Sammy stared at her. He had never known a little kid who took care of sick grown-ups. Etta Jean had taken care of two. He had always had his parents to care for him. It was hard for him to realize how many problems Etta Jean had had.

"She got a lot worse after I started school in third grade. Grandma couldn't wash my clothes or cook or take care of me. And one time...one time..." Etta Jean turned her face away from Sammy and he had to strain to hear what she said. "That girl, you know Angela, that helped me a lot in school, well, she told me I was dirty and stunk and she wouldn't help me anymore. The kids wouldn't play with me. I did so bad with my school stuff they called me stupid. I didn't go to school for a while then."

Sammy was shocked. "Why, that's awful that you didn't go to school. Kindergarten was fun. That girl shouldn't have told you that you stunk." Sammy stomped his feet as he walked back and forth. "I hate that girl that was mean to you, Etta Jean. I won't be mean to you."

Etta Jean turned to him and smiled. "Don't hate Angela, Sammy. She kinda taught me when she said that. I asked Mrs. Lyons and she told me how to wash clothes and how much soap and everything. I put our clothes in the washer and dryer myself. I'd take baths, and washed my hair when we had shampoo, and put on clean clothes. Then I was clean and Angela and the other kids liked me again."

"Wow. You washed your own clothes." Sammy was impressed.

"Yeah," Etta Jean hopped off the picnic table. "And my grandma's clothes, too. I had to tell Grandma to take baths and get dressed. I even had to tell her to go to bed at night."

"How'd you eat?" Sammy stopped and listened carefully.

"Well, my grandma got a check every month. I would have her sign the check at home then I would lead her to the bank and have her cash the check. Then I put the money in a little coin purse. I learned a lot. I would take money to that one store and pay for electricity and water there. Then I would try to save as much as I could to buy milk and lunchmeat and potato chips and sometimes apples and once in a great while I'd have enough money to buy a little carton of ice cream. Both my grandma and I liked ice cream. We didn't have it much though." She looked around and then smoothed out a dirty pile of dirt Sammy had made with his toe.

"You mean you didn't have anything to eat unless you bought it yourself? My mommy and sometimes my dad buy us stuff to eat. We always have yots."

Etta Jean sneezed. "Well, sometimes Grandma Etta and I didn't have much to eat at all."

Sammy stared at her. To not have enough to eat was hard to believe.

Etta Jean looked up. "Listen, Sammy. Listen to those birds sing. And look. There's a cardinal. It's singing. It's so pretty." Etta Jean smiled. "They make me so happy!" She laughed her deep laugh.

Birds singing makes her happy, Sammy thought, when she didn't even have ice cream very much. Sammy shook his head and made a dirt pile out of the smooth place she had made, and then he smoothed out all the dirt piles. "That's awful that you had to do all that, Etta Jean. It's awful that you couldn't have ice cream when you wanted it. We always have it."

Etta Jean nodded and stared off into the distance. "Aw, not so bad. What was hardest was that Grandma had this disease that made her forget a lot. She didn't mean to forget." Etta Jean reached down and retied her shoelace.

"Then what happened," Sammy asked staring at her.

"Well, Grandma Etta got worse. One time she was trying to cook something and had the stove on, and flames started shooting up. I grabbed a dish towel, got the pan, and threw it outside."

"And now you're ain't living with your grandma. Did your grandma burn your house?"

"Mr. Lyons said she was trying to cook and forgot. She didn't mean to burn the house, Sammy. It was an accident. I went to buy some milk and apples, and someone told me to run home, that our house was on fire. But I had to run five blocks and it was all burning when I got there." Etta Jean turned to Sammy. "You saw me when my grandma's house burned."

"Yeah." Sammy clutched her sleeve. "Did your grandma get on fire?"

"No, she went over to Lyon's when our house got on fire." Etta Jean took a deep breath. "I wish I'd been home to take the pan that caught on fire or whatever it was outside."

"You did run into the house," Sammy shook his head at her. "You could have burned up."

"I had to, Sammy. I had to get this picture of my mom. It's the best thing I have. If the fireman hadn't made me leave so fast I might have got some clothes. Also I had a doll and two books, that I wished I had grabbed."

A doll and two books? Were those all the toys his friend had? He thought about the piles of toys in his closet and in the basement. "Where's your grandma now?"

"I told you. Don't you listen? She's in a nursing home. I don't know where or which one. I hope my grandma is all right. I'd like to go see her." Etta Jean sighed and turned her head away. She spoke so softly Sammy almost didn't hear her. "I hope they're taking good care of Grandma."

"So you went to your stepfather's?"

"Yeah. Mr. Lyons drove me there. My stepfather's got a new wife and she's got two kids. They said I had to sleep on the floor. They gave me an old quilt to lay on, but I got cold and had to cover up with it and just laid on the floor. The cushion they gave me for a pillow smelled bad. I heard them talking."

Etta Jean stopped talking for so long, Sammy began to think she was mad at him.

She walked a few steps toward the street and then back again. "They didn't want me. They said I couldn't stay there—I knew my stepfather wouldn't want me." Etta Jean looked down and her face was sad.

Etta Jean walked fast around the picnic table. She folded her hands over and over each other. Sammy knew she was upset. She walked over to a tree still wringing her hands and took about three deep breaths. Finally she stopped and came back.

When she stopped, Sammy was glad to see the sad look was gone from her face.

"Come on, Sammy. Let's walk around and look at people. I want to see what they're eating."

Sammy wanted to stop and play on the swings again, but Etta Jean took his hand and pulled him on. They walked around the picnic area and sauntered over where a family was eating. She motioned him to sit on the grass with her behind a tree, where she could watch the family.

"We'll stay here for a while," she whispered. She held her finger up to her lips, and Sammy was quiet.

After the family finished eating, the woman put their leftover food in a plastic bag then shoved it in a garbage can. When the family walked away, Etta Jean hurried over and pulled out the plastic bag. "Look! There's four whole pieces of chicken that nobody even bit into. And almost a whole bag of potato chips. And six cookies. Chocolate chip. I like them! Wow! Look! There's three apples. Oh, boy, ain't we lucky!" Etta Jean was smiling and excited as she pulled small clean plastic bags from her backpack and put food in them. She dumped chicken bones and the rest of the trash back in the garbage can.

Sammy ran to a nearby picnic table and sat on a bench. He was so hungry, he could hardly wait for her to bring the food to him.

Etta Jean came and sat on the bench across from him and handed Sammy one piece of chicken, the bag of potato chips and one cookie, laying out the same amount for her, then stowed the rest in her backpack.

"This will be our supper," she laughed her deep laugh.

"I wanna go home. I want to see Mommy and Daddy. I don't like eating out of garbage cans," Sammy whined. "You didn't give me enough to eat."

"Listen, Sammy. I don't know how to get you home, but I'll try to find out tomorrow. I don't like to get food out of garbage cans to eat either, but I don't have any money to buy you food. You don't have any money either. It's better to eat out of garbage cans than be hungry. Stop whining."

'You're awful bossy, Etta Jean."

"Yeah, sometimes I am." She bit into the chicken. "So good," she murmured.

Sammy shrugged and ate more than his share of potato chips. After eating they went to the fountain and took turns drinking cool water at the fountain. They played on the swings, stopped by the bathrooms twice, drank again at the water fountain, walked around, looked at the flowers, and talked some more.

"What have you been doing since you've been lost, Sammy?"

"At the rest stop this big woman's pants were all tearing and I could see her underpants," Sammy giggled. "I accidentally tripped the girl that was with her. She hit me and I hit her back. She chased me and I hid. Then I spit on her shoes."

Etta Jean laughed and laughed her deep belly laugh

"You really spit on her shoes?"

"No, I missed." He shrugged. "She went back where her mother was."

Etta Jean laughed some more. "I like being with you, Sammy," she said.

"How are you gonna get me home tomorrow?" Sammy asked.

"I don't know. I'm thinking. We'll get you home."

"Well, I sure hope so," Sammy whispered. "I gotta get home for my bertday on Saturday! I gotta, Etta Jean…"

—

Chapter Fourteen - Wednesday Evening

It was getting late. Sammy was hungry and tired. He stumbled and muttered "Clinker Dab!"

"What did you say?" Etta Jean asked.

"I said Clinker Dab. When I stumbled, I hurt my toe."

"Clinker Dab," Etta Jean repeated. "Clinker Dab. That's the funniest words I ever heard," she laughed her deep belly laugh. They slowly trudged the four blocks back to the alley and cardboard house home.

"How did you find this place?"

"Well, after I heard my step-dad tell his wife that no way would he let me stay there, and that on Monday he would take me to the courts and have me put in foster care, I left."

Sammy listened. All these new things he was hearing about were new to him.

Etta opened the flaps of the cardboard box and sighed. "It was dark and late at night, but I grabbed my backpack and went outside and down the street. I thought maybe that nice girl at school—Angela would let me stay at her house for a couple of days. I didn't know where she lived though." Etta Jean pulled the little picture out of her backpack, looked at it, and smiled. "My mother was so pretty," she whispered.

"What's foster care?"

"That's where they put kids that don't have homes. Two girls that were in my class were in foster care. They came to school with bruises that they showed me when we were in the bathroom."

"Why didn't those girls go someplace else?"

"I don't know. Maybe they did later. I hope they got a nice place to stay, but I was really scared when I heard my stepfather say he would take me to foster care." Etta Jean straightened out some of the newspapers that were on the floor or bed of the cardboard box.

"I was walking down the street late and it was dark Sunday night. I was crying, and Hank saw me. He said I shouldn't be on the street and to go home. I told him I didn't have any place to go, so he walked with me quite a long way, then we came to this place and he found this big cardboard box. He got a blanket and some newspapers for me to lie on. I've been lonesome, but it's really kinda cozy with you here, and having some one to talk with. Hank works when he can and Kate won't talk." She smiled. "I saw you Monday morning. Remember?"

"Yeah, I remember. What were you doing there?"

"Well, I thought maybe Angela would come to the store and I could ask her if I could stay with her. I stayed around all day, but I didn't see her. Then I decided she wouldn't let me stay. Her mother wouldn't want me either."

"What did you eat?"

"Oh, I just about got in trouble," Etta Jean laughed. "Somebody left a big piece of pizza on the table and walked away. I thought it was to be thrown away, so I got it and went over to a corner table and was eating it when the man came back and looked for his pizza. He'd just gone over for coffee. I was embarrassed. You should have seen the look on that man's face, Sammy, when he couldn't find his pizza." Etta Jean laughed her deep bubbling laugh, and Sammy laughed, too.

"Sammy, that pizza was so good. It was all I had on Monday to eat. Hank told me about Andy who sometimes sneaks out food for him at McDonalds, so I went there yesterday morning. Hank told him I would be coming, so he was watching for me. Andy talks mean sometimes, but he's really awfully nice."

117

Sammy thought about all the good food his mother prepared for him. It made him more and more homesick. He huddled in a corner with his knees up and looked around. "There's nothing to do," he whined.

She smiled. "We can talk. It's better having you here than being alone."

"You don't have any TV or video games or nothing. It's just an old box without windows and it's dark in here."

"Well, Sammy, I wish I had a place to live. That's for sure. I wish I had a better place for you to visit me. If I had, I'd sure take you to it." Etta Jean rubbed her eyes and forehead. She sat with her head down.

"It smells in this alley. Smells like old banana peels and spoiled onions and bad smells like a bathroom has some times." Sammy held his nose.

Etta Jean lowered her head more and stared at her worn, dingy shoes. "I'm sorry, Sammy."

Sammy watched her for a moment and felt sorry for Etta Jean who had no home. He reached out and touched her sleeve. He wanted to hug her, like his mother hugged him, but he didn't.

"It's all right, Etta Jean. I yike being with you."

She smiled. "Yeah. Sammy, when it smells bad I think of good smells. One time Mrs. Lyon brought over a skillet of fried potatoes and onions. Oh, they were good and smelled wonderful. Grandma and I ate the whole big skillet full." Etta Jean giggled remembering. "She told me how to fix them and I fixed them sometimes for Grandma and me. And one time Mrs. Lyons brought us a big plate of oatmeal cookies with raisins. I kept one of mine on the table in the living room, close to where I slept, so I could smell it all night."

The flap of the cardboard box 'door' was abruptly jerked open. "Did you kids eat today?" Hank asked. "I worked unloading a truck and they paid me. I kin get you kids something to eat."

"Thanks, Hank, but we've ate good," Etta Jean told him. "Wait a minute." She pulled out an apple and two cookies. "Here's an apple and a cookie for you and a cookie for Kate."

"Well, thanks, Etta Jean. You're a mighty fine gal. Kate'll like having a cookie," Hank said pushing the flap shut as he left.

"I wanted those cookies, Etta Jean," Sammy whined.

She looked at him for a long moment. "You'll have lots of cookies when you go home. Here we share. Last night I wouldn't have had anything to eat if Hank hadn't brought me a cheese sandwich and a cup of water."

Etta Jean handed him a piece of chicken, the few potato chips that were left, and a cookie. "We don't have anything to drink, but when we eat the apples, it will just be like drinking water," she smiled.

Sammy got through eating first. After they ate, she wrapped their apple cores and chicken bones in a piece of newspaper. "We'll walk up to that gas station and throw this in the trash and use the bathrooms to wash our hands."

"It's two blocks away and I'm tired," Sammy whined.

"So you got a better idea?" She crawled out and Sammy followed.

After they returned, Etta Jean giggled. "I have a game we can play." She showed Sammy how to play a light hand slapping hand game made more difficult by changing and moving hands. The children played. Sammy laughed a lot, and Etta Jean laughed her deep-throated laugh over and over.

When they tired of the game and leaned back in the corners of the cardboard box, Etta Jean said, "Sammy—I'll never forget you. It's so much fun having you here. Like I told you, the kids at school—when I got to go—don't play with me much. I never looked nice, and I didn't do well with my lessons, 'cause I missed school. Sammy, I really like it because you're being nice to me."

Sammy was thoughtful. This girl was different than anyone he ever knew. "Etta Jean," he asked quietly, "do you have any toys?"

"Yeah, Sammy. I had that pretty doll I told you about and two books. I had clothes, too. Not many, but some. My mother had me keep the doll that Grandma gave me hid under the couch when my step-dad was home because he broke my other doll that time. When my grandma came over and got me, I had the doll to take to her house. Grandma Etta liked me to play with it and even made it a new dress before she started forgetting. She bought me two books and a game and clothes when she felt good. I still had the two books and the doll, but they burned."

"I have yots of toys," Sammy said then wished he hadn't said that.

Etta Jean didn't act like it made her feel bad though. She smiled at him. "I'd like to see them."

Sammy yawned.

"I'll fix our bed, Sammy. It gets cool at night, even though Hank gave me a lot of newspapers to sleep on. My blanket isn't very big, but we can share it. You lie down and put your back to me with your head next to my waist. That way they'll be enough blanket to cover us both."

Sammy did as he was told and Etta Jean carefully tucked the blanket around him. He tried to go to sleep, but kept wishing he were home. The pavement was hard under the newspapers and bottom of the cardboard box. He didn't have a pillow and tried to lie with his head on his arm. He thought about his soft bed but mostly about his mother and daddy. He started crying.

"Now, Sammy, don't cry for your Mom and Dad. I told you I've been thinking. In the morning I'll ask Hank for money to use the 'phone. We'll call them and they'll come get you."

Sammy didn't want to admit he was crying for his parents. "I'm not crying for my mommy. My feet are cold," Sammy lied. He sniffed loudly several times.

Etta Jean got up and took off her dirty tennis shoes and her ragged blue socks. She untied and pulled off Sammy's expensive Reeboks then pulled her warm socks on over Sammy's. "Now put your shoes on and you'll feel warmer."

She reached under a corner of the newspapers and pulled out a grayish pair of socks with so many holes Sammy couldn't see how they would keep her feet warm. "Hank found these and gave them to me," she said.

Sammy pulled on his shoes as he watched her. Finally she got on her ragged socks and worn out shoes.

Sammy lay there for a while. He knew the blanket didn't cover her shoulders and she had no jacket. He sat up, took off his jacket, crawled up, and put it around Etta Jean's shoulders. She took hold of his hand just for an instant and gave him a big smile.

Sammy lay back down, pulled the blanket up, and smiled.

Sammy wiggled into the newspapers a little more. He was warm under the blanket and his feet were warm. She had given him her blanket and would have slept cold if he hadn't remembered to give her his jacket.

Would Sybil have done that for him? No, he decided. Would he have given up a blanket for Etta Jean. No, probably not. But now that he had met Etta Jean and saw how giving she was, maybe he would have. She was like not anybody he ever knew.

"Etta Jean," he whispered. "You asleep?"

"Not quite," she whispered back.

"Thanks, Etta Jean. Thanks."

"That's OK, Sammy," she said..

He heard a deep chuckle. He smiled.

"Tell me again, Larry, about the truck driver," Emily said holding Sammy's soiled red shirt.

"Lt. Sloan said a truck driver telephoned the police Wednesday morning in Atlanta and asked if the small red-haired boy was back with his parents in Flint, Michigan. The policeman who answered had just heard a report that he was not home yet. The truck driver said he saw him at a rest stop north of Dayton, Ohio, Tuesday morning and told him to go to a police car and the police would see that he got home."

"How did Sammy get there—almost to Dayton?"

"That the police don't know. Later Sloan telephoned me again. They checked and there was a police car at the rest stop about the time the truck driver saw Sammy, but the police didn't see him. Emily, we know he was safe and well Tuesday morning. Keep that in mind. The police are checking in that area. It's just a shame the driver waited until Wednesday to call."

Emily said a silent prayer of thanksgiving that Sammy was safe on Tuesday morning. Now it was Wednesday night and she prayed

124

quietly that he would soon be home. She saw Larry's tense, worried face. They had to think all the time that their precious boy would be all right.

"Larry, remember that Easter when Sammy said Santa Claus was coming to bring him a candy bar?"

"Yes. He said that Santa Claus would put the candy bar in a wastebasket instead of an Easter basket. He certainly got that mixed up."

Emily smiled. "We didn't correct him because we thought it was so cute."

They talked more of happy times. The days of anguish had kept Larry and Emily from sleeping well for several nights. Tonight the pleasant remembrances relaxed them a little. Before Emily went to bed, she put the Sammy's soiled red shirt close to her face on the pillow. She folded her hands. "Thank you, thank you, God for keeping Sammy safe and that we know where he was yesterday morning. Wherever Sammy is tonight, please let him be with someone kind who will care for him and see that he is warm."

But is he warm? Is someone kind looking after him?

—

Chapter Fifteen - Thursday Morning

When Sammy woke up, he saw Etta Jean sitting near the open 'door' flaps of the cardboard box, trying to comb her long, wavy hair with a broken piece of a pink comb. Sunshine made the box much brighter. Sammy wiggled his nose. The alley smelled badly of rotten garbage and bathroom smells, but he didn't want to say anything that would hurt Etta Jean's feelings.

"Hi, Etta Jean," he said as he wiggled out from under the torn blanket.

"Hi, Sammy." She smiled at him. "I like having you here. It's awful lonesome to wake up and have nobody to talk to me."

Sammy smiled back. He took off his shoes and her worn socks, then put his shoes back on. He watched her struggle with her hair. "I'll comb your hair for you, Etta Jean," Sammy said. He knelt behind her, took the comb, and tried to get out the tangles. He worked several minutes. Her hair was so snarled and the piece of comb was so little, that he found it very hard to get her hair smooth.

"That feels good, Sammy. Nobody's combed my hair for a long time," Etta Jean turned and smiled at him. She took the socks he had worn, folded them neatly, and tucked them under newspapers in a corner.

"Didn't your grandma comb your hair?"

"Well, yes, she did at first. She had trouble combing it and said it was too much trouble. One time she got scissors and cut off a lot of my hair. Etta Jean turned and smiled at Sammy. "Can you braid my hair like my mother used to braid it?"

"What's braid?"

"Well, you divide my hair in three parts, then lay one over the others."

"I can't do that. I don't know what you're talking about." He was quiet for a few minutes. "Etta Jean," Sammy found it hard to tell her. "I wasn't crying last night 'cause my feet were cold. I cried 'cause I want to go home awful bad and be with my mommy and daddy. I yike being with you. Honest, Etta Jean, but I want to go home." He quit fighting the battle with he tangles in Etta Jean's long hair and gave her back the piece of broken comb.

127

"I know you want to go home, Sammy, and today I'll help you." She tucked the broken comb back into her backpack.

"Next time we're at a store, I'm staying close to my parents, and I'm never gonna say that I'm going with my mommy when I'm supposed to be with my daddy." Sammy sat down with his hands on his knees and legs stretched out straight. His shoulders slumped and his fists clenched. He looked at Etta Jean and couldn't keep back the tears. "I wanta go home!"

"Don't cry, Sammy. You'll get home. I'll take care of you and help you." Etta Jean folded the ragged blanket neatly and stuffed it in her backpack. "You know you're awfully lucky to have parents and a home." Etta Jean turned away and sniffed.

"I wish you had a home, Etta Jean. A real home," he wiped tears away on his jacket sleeves.

"I wish I did, too, Sammy. Sometimes I cry in the night. Sometimes I try to pray like Mama taught me to pray." Etta Jean gave a big sigh. "I prayed that Mama would get better, but she died. I prayed that my grandma wouldn't forget so much, but she forgot more." Etta Jean tried to straighten some of the rumpled newspapers. "I tried to pray the last few nights for a real home. Either I don't know how to pray right, or God doesn't like me." Etta Jean smiled and shrugged her shoulders.

"I prayed for you. The night after we saw the house burning, I asked Mommy if you had a place to sleep and she didn't know but said I should pray for you. So I did." Sammy raised his shoulders and grinned.

"You prayed for me? Wow. Nobody's prayed for me since my mother. Maybe my grandma did before she started having her little strokes. Wow." Her smile was broad and radiant. "That's cool, Sammy."

"Etta Jean, maybe you could come home with me and be my sister. My mother would comb your hair. She'd braid it and everything."

"Be your sister?" Etta Jean laughed her deep, belly laugh. "In your dreams. I can't be your sister. You're a crazy boy."

"Yeah, sure you can. That's what I wanted for my bertday—a sister. Mommy will buy you new clothes and we have good food at home. My dad and I yike chocolate mint ice cream. We almost always have some," Sammy grinned.

129

Etta Jean laughed. "It'll never happen. Your mom and dad won't want me. They'll be just like my stepfather. You know that neighbor lady I told you about? Mrs. Lyons? The neighbor who brought us cookies and fried potatoes and onions? Well, I wasn't going to tell anybody this, but you're my friend and I'll tell you. When my grandma's house was burning, and Mrs. Lyon said my grandma would have to go to a nursing home, I asked her if I could live with her."

"What did she say?"

"She said..." Etta Jean's head was down and it was hard for Sammy to hear her. "She said that she'd raised her kids and couldn't raise any more. She said I'd be just fine. But I haven't been. Nobody wants me, Sammy." Etta Jean looked down for a few minutes, and was very quiet. Sammy didn't know what to say or do.

He was glad when she raised her head and smiled at Sammy. "But somehow I'll find a place to live and I'll be OK." She smiled again.

Sammy watched Etta Jean tie back her hair with the twisted bit of yellow ribbon.

Emily carelessly pulled her hair into a ponytail.

"I like your hair that way, Emily. It shows the back of your beautiful neck," Larry said dropping a kiss on her smooth, white neck.

"Well, it's easy to fix," she met his eyes in the mirror. "Larry, you know I always dreamed that when our baby daughter grew older, I would braid her hair, or put it in a ponytail, or sometimes curl it. I dreamed about buying clothes and dolls for a baby girl. I even planned her red velvet Christmas dress. Sometimes when I see a pretty dress for a baby girl in a store window or even something for a little girl's hair, I can't keep the tears back. It's great fun to buy toys and clothes for Sammy and I am grateful we can do that." She paused as she put on lipstick. "It would be great for Sammy to have a sister."

Larry's eyes misted. Here his wife was talking about having two children, and they might not even have one. He walked across the room and stared out the window. "We'll go back to the adoption agency. Someday we'll have a baby sister for Sammy. I promise," he said in a husky voice that was barely in control.

Emily picked up the red shirt and held it to her cheek. "We have a child now. I so want him home. Sammy, Sammy," she whispered.

131

Etta Jean smiled as she reached into her backpack, dug around, and brought out the picture of her and her mother. She gazed at it for a moment and smiled.

"Leave that stuff here, Etta Jean. I'm awful hungry and I got to go to the bathroom. We'll come back later and get it. Hurry."

"I take my backpack wherever I go, Sammy. It's all I have." She kissed the picture then carefully placed it back in her backpack.

"You kissed that ole picture. You're not supposed to kiss pictures," Sammy told her. "You're supposed to kiss people."

"I'd kiss my grandma if I could see her. After I get you home, the next thing I do is find my grandma. I want to see her."

"Well, you ain't kissing me!" Sammy quickly crawled out of the box and ran down the alley.

"And I sure don't want to!" Etta Jean laughed her deep laugh as she caught up with him.

At the office building Etta Jean told him, "Now you wash good. Your hands look dirty."

"You don't have to tell me what to do. You ain't my mother," Sammy called back as he went into the men's bathroom where he did wash his hands thoroughly and splashed water on his face.

Sammy followed Etta Jean to McDonalds and watched her wave as they passed the window. Sammy couldn't help fidgeting, while Etta Jean sat patiently as they waited. This time the pimply faced teenage brought two cheeseburgers, two cartons of milk and two cups of orange juice.

"Thanks, Andy. That's sure nice of you to bring us milk and orange juice both," Etta Jean smiled at him and Sammy felt her poke him with her elbow.

"Thank you, Andy," he said and smiled, too. Sometimes Sammy wished he could be as nice as Etta Jean.

Going back to the office building they sat on the steps and ate. Etta Jean saved her cup of juice and insisted Sammy save his. They went back into the office building bathrooms and threw the trash into the wastebaskets.

"Let's go find Hank and see if he's got money so we can phone Mommy," Sammy was almost jumping up and down he was so eager to call his mother.

"Before you woke up, I heard Hank leaving for work. He's loading a truck again today. I ran after him, and I got the money to call," Etta Jean laughed. "I was gonna surprise you. I know you want to go home, but I'll miss you, Sammy."

"After I go home what will you do, Etta Jean? You can't stay in that cardboard box. What if Andy won't give you breakfast anymore? How will you eat?"

She didn't answer. He knew she didn't know. He stared at her for a moment then urged, "Come on, yet's call my parents."

—

Chapter Sixteen - Thursday Mid-Day

"Come on. I saw a 'phone at that gas station. Let's call Mommy."

He ran down the sidewalk and Etta Jean followed until they got to the

telephone located on a pole near the gas station.

Sammy couldn't reach it. "You'll have to call, Etta Jean."

"Hold my cup of juice. What's your number?"

"It's 349-6890."

Etta Jean could barely reach the telephone. By stretching a lot she

could manage. "Now you'll soon be home," she smiled at Sammy.

Dropping the coin into the slot, she said, "349. What's the rest of it?"

Sammy stood by hopping from one foot to the other. Soon he

would be talking to his mother. "6890."

"6809," Etta Jean said as she punched the buttons.

"No. No. It's 6890, Etta Jean. Oh, no."

"Is this Sammy's mother?" Etta Jean asked. She waited a moment

then said, "Is this 349-6890?" Her face fell in disappointment. "They

said 'wrong number' and hung up." She quietly hung up the receiver

and turned to face Sammy.

"Oh, Etta Jean! Clinker Dab! You stupid—you dork! You turkey! You—you dialed the wrong number. You yost the money. I'll never, never want you for my sister. Now I can't go home." Sammy walked to the curb, sat down, put down the cups of juice, and put his hands to his face and sobbed.

"I'm sorry, Sammy, I'm sorry." Etta Jean said over and over. She put her arm across his shoulders. "I'm sorry. We'll find some money. We will. We'll call again. It will be all right, Sammy." She wrung her hands. "I'm sorry."

She sat quietly beside him. When his crying became hiccuping sobs, Etta Jean opened his cup of juice and handed it to him. He took sips between sobs. Etta Jean opened hers and drank. After they drank all their juice, she dumped the empty cups in a wastebasket.

"We'll go back to the alley, Sammy. Maybe Kate would give us some money. It will be all right, Sammy." She patted his arm.

Before they got to the alley, they met Kate pushing her grocery cart fast and not counting or pausing with her foot lifted. "Run, run, kids, get away," she said in a loud voice. "They're going to be after us. Now run."

"Can we have some money, Mrs...." Sammy ran after her.

Kate did not turn or look at him but kept walking away very fast.

He turned and looked at Etta Jean who stared after Kate with a strange look on her face.

"Who's gonna be after us?" Sammy asked.

"I don't know," Etta Jean said over her shoulder as she ran ahead. Sammy hurried after her. When they started in the alley, Etta Jean stopped suddenly and Sammy ran into her. Both stood with open mouths as they watched Etta Jean's cardboard box being tossed into a garbage truck.

"No. No. My home. Now what am I going to do? I won't have any place to sleep tonight. Oh, no." Etta Jean ran a few steps after the garbage truck. "Give me back my box," she shouted but the men on the truck didn't hear her.

"What'll I do, Sammy? Where will I go? What'll I do?" She ran a few steps then stopped and wrung her hands.

Hank came out of the alley. "I saw the garbage truck coming this way, so ran down here, but I was too late to save our boxes. Etta, you go and take the boy with you. They'll pick us all up if we stay around here. Wait a day or two, then come back if you don't have another place to stay, girl, and I'll try to find you something. Now get away

137

from here, kids. Quick." He gave them a little shove. "I have to go back to work," he said as he turned and rushed away. "Go!"

Etta Jean and Sammy ran. They ran and ran, past the park and kept going. Out of breath they stopped and leaned against a car.

Sammy was shocked to see Etta Jean with tears running down her cheeks. "I forgot to ask Hank for more money to call. I don't know where he works."

"Don't cry, Etta Jean, don't cry. I'm not mad at you anymore."

"How could I mix up your number? I'm a dork. I'm stupid like you said," Etta Jean started sobbing. "The kids at school called me stupid. I am stupid. I don't have anything or anywhere to sleep. I don't even have those other socks. All I have is my old blanket, my mother's picture, my comb, and a few clean plastic bags that Hank gave me. That's all I have." "I'm sorry, Etta Jean. I'm sorry." Sammy went to her. He wiped her tears away with his hand and patted her arm. "Don't cry, Etta Jean. I don't want you to cry. Please don't cry." He thought about hugging her, but was afraid she would shove him away.

"Where are we gonna sleep? "Etta Jean grabbed his hand still crying. "I'm trying to take care of you. I'm trying real hard. I don't know what will happen to us. If we get a long way from that office building where will I wash? What am I gonna do?" Etta Jean sobbed and sobbed.

Sammy tried to hug her but she had her hands up to her face. "I'll take care of you, Etta Jean. You're gonna be my sister. I didn't mean what I said about not wanting you to be my sister. We'll walk till we come to my house. You'll really be my sister." He patted her shoulder. He patted her arm. He patted her hand.

"I wish I could, Sammy. How I wish I could! But I know your parents won't want me. They'll be just like Mrs. Lyon. When you go home, I'll be lonesome 'cause you've been nice to me." She wiped her nose on the bottom of her green shirt. Now she was the one who was having hiccuping sobs.

"Come on. We'll walk. My house is that way 'cause the sun shines in the kitchen windows in the afternoon and it's to our backs now. Come on." Sammy took her arm and helped her along.

Finally her sobs stopped. "Sammy, if I could be your sister, I'd help your mother. I'd wash clothes and dust and clean. I'd work hard just to be able to stay in your house." Her shoulders slumped. "But they won't want me. Let's not talk about it anymore. I'll get you

139

home then I'll find someplace." She wiped her eyes with her hands and her nose again with the bottom of her sweatshirt. She was trying hard to quit crying.

"Where will you find someplace to live?"

"I don't know!" Etta Jean's voice sounded cross. "I wish I knew!"

A police car drove by, then stopped and backed up. Frightened, Sammy grabbed her hand. They ran up a driveway and around a house.

"The police could get you home, Sammy. What are you doin'?"

"They'll 'rest me cause I stole stuff."

"Yeah, it's bad to steal stuff. But I don't think they'd arrest you."

"Yes, they will," Sammy said as he pulled Etta Jean down to hide behind some shrubbery. When he saw the police car drive away, Sammy was still scared. "We'll walk in behind these houses," he said.

When they started across the street Sammy saw the police car coming back and took her hand again. They ran behind a house and hid by an air conditioner. Sammy knelt but Etta Jean sat down.

"Can we go now?" Etta Jean said. "I'm sitting on a rock and it hurts."

Sammy giggled as she squinted her eyes and wrinkled her nose.

She slid off the rock and laughed her deep laugh and then stretched out on her back. Sammy stretched out beside her and they both laughed. They started to get up, then fell back and laughed some more.

"Whoever lives in this house will see us and think we're crazy," Etta Jean laughed.

Soon they went back to the sidewalk and walked on. Although they looked at every house on both sides of the street, Sammy would shake his head when Etta Jean would point to one.

About an hour later still walking Etta Jean confided, "You know last night, Sammy, I dreamed about living in a real house where I didn't have to worry about finding something to eat. I dreamed about living with people that weren't mean or sick and who liked me. Who really liked me! That would be nice."

Sammy leaned over and put his arm around her shoulder. "You'll be my sister, Etta Jean. I know it. You won't have to take care of me anymore. Mommy and Daddy'll take care of both of us. You'll have your own room in the room that Mommy fixed up for the baby that didn't come home with us." He tenderly touched her cheek, pulled his arm away, and stepped back.

Etta Jean put her fingers up to her cheek where Sammy touched her and smiled. "I'll have my own room? With my own bed? I never had my own room. When Mommy was alive she slept with my stepfather and I slept in a crib in the same room. Then when my stepfather had us move to that little apartment, he sold the crib and I slept on the couch in the living room."

"Where'd you sleep when you yived with your grandma?"

"On the couch in the living room. Where else?"

"Your grandma's house looked bigger than that."

"Yeah, it had three bedrooms, but Grandma had one fixed up with chairs and a desk and where she watched TV, and then she had her quilting frames and paint stuff in the other room. Did I tell you Grandma painted pictures? When I came to live with her, she said she'd buy me a bed and fix one of the rooms for me, then she got to forgetting." Etta Jean took Sammy's hand for a moment. "I sure want to find my grandma and see if she's all right. I worry about her. She loves me and I love her."

Sammy was thinking. What if his parents didn't want her. "Etta Jean, when school starts how are you gonna go to school?"

"Well, one time Hank said maybe I could live with his mother."

142

"Why aren't you living with her now?"

"She's sick. Maybe she'll be well when it's time to go to school." Etta Jean sighed again. "I don't know, Sammy. I don't know where I'll live or nothin'. Quit asking questions." Etta Jean straightened the old backpack on her back and trudged ahead. She blew out a long breath.

"What about Mrs. Lyons?" Sammy said softly.

Etta Jean stopped and patted his hand. "I could stay with her for a week or two, I know. She's nice. She cuts my bangs sometimes. You've been nice. I'll never forget you, Sammy. And how you prayed for me. But I'll never be your sister and you know it."

The children were quiet as they walked on with Sammy looking carefully at every house they passed. They walked for about two hours.

"Are you sure we're going the right way."

Sammy stopped and looked around. "Yeah. We yive out this way." He pointed ahead.

"O.K. We'll walk that way 'til we find them," Etta Jean smiled at him. She squared her shoulders and took off at a fast walk.

They walked and walked and walked. Two more hours passed and they trudged very slowly.

"I'm tired, Etta Jean. Yet's rest a while." The children sat on a curb.

"Do these houses look like those by your mom and dad?"

"Yeah. No. I don't know. I'm awful tired." The children rested.

"What day is today, Etta Jean?"

"I don't know. What does your paper say?"

He pulled the worn paper out of his pocket. "It's another 'T,' so…" it

"It's Thursday," Etta Jean said.

"Yeah. Sure. I knew it all the time," Sammy made his X. "Now it's only one day after today until my bertday," he perked up. "And I'll get what I want for my bertday—a sister—you." Sammy smiled at her.

Etta Jean didn't return his smile. She looked down and the expression on her face was the saddest Sammy had ever seen. "It'll never happen, Sammy." She got up from the curb and started walking and Sammy followed.

144

The string holding Etta Jean's shoe together broke and there wasn't enough left to get her shoe tied again. It was difficult for her to walk because her shoe kept sliding off. A couple of tears slid down her cheeks.

A car driving by slowed and a teenage girl yelled," You two stupid kids get out of this neighborhood. You're dirty and grungy."

Etta Jean turned and faced Sammy. "Do I look awful, Sammy? Do I look grungy? Tell me."

Sammy looked at her ragged dirty green sweatshirt and pants, her tangled hair that he wasn't able to comb with the piece of comb, her worn tennis shoes with one falling part way off her foot. Then he looked at her sweet face with its pert nose, full lips, and pretty eyes. He touched her cheek lightly with his forefinger. "You're not grungy. You're pretty, Etta Jean. You're real pretty."

Etta Jean smiled. They walked on. Then her shoe fell off and she sat down to put it on. Once again she tried to tie the string together, but it broke again. She got up and tried to walk. It was hard for her to keep her shoe on her foot. They walked about three blocks and every step was a struggle for her.

145

They stopped again and Sammy pulled up his pants. He was having a hard time keeping his jeans pulled up. "I'm awful hungry and thirsty," he whined. "And I gotta go to the bathroom."

"Your jeans are getting too loose. You don't get enough to eat," Etta Jean told him. "I'm not taking good care of you. And I don't know what we're gonna do?" She started crying then began sobbing loudly.

By now the sun shone on their faces as they walked west. "I'm so hungry, too. I don't know where to get anything to eat. I don't know what to do," she said between sobs. Her sobs got louder and louder.

Sammy looked around in panic. He didn't want the car with the teen-age girl to drive by and yell bad things at them again. Etta Jean was sobbing louder. What should he do? He pushed and pulled her into the backyard of a house and on to the backyard of the next house. Tall pine trees and shrubs separated the two houses and Etta Jean fell exhausted to the grass.

Sammy knelt beside her and patted her shoulder. He dug in his pocket for his flashlight. Her sobs continued to shake her shoulders. Sammy took the perfume bottle from his other pocket, pulled her hands from her face and put the perfume bottle in one hand.

"Don't cry, Etta Jean. Don't cry. Please don't. Here. Take these." He tried to push the flashlight into her other hand.

Etta Jean tried to stop crying. She tried to smile at Sammy, but the tears continued to roll. "Where did you get these, Sammy. I never saw them before."

"I accidentally stole them. But I'll have my mommy pay for them when I get home. I hid them under the newspapers when we slept last night," he explained. "Please take these, Etta Jean," he coaxed. He patted her arm. "Please."

She looked up at him through her tears. "I can't take these, Sammy. They're yours."

"They're for you. Please stop crying. Put them in your backpack."

"Then you won't have anything, Sammy."

"Yes, I do. I got you," he smiled at her.

Etta Jean pulled up the bottom of her sweatshirt and wiped her nose and eyes.

"Are you really giving these to me, Sammy?"

"Yeah. Sure."

"Thank you, Sammy," Etta Jean whispered and took the flashlight and perfume bottle. "I haven't had any presents for a long time." She

147

smiled her radiant smile. "Well, I have the blanket Hank gave me but these are nicer presents." She turned the flashlight off and on and opened the perfume bottle and smelled it but didn't put any on. She hugged Sammy. "Thank you. I'll remember you always. I'll remember how I had to tell you to wash." She wiped her eyes and nose again with the bottom of her sweatshirt and tried to smile, then she put the flashlight and perfume deep in her backpack.

When they heard a door slam and people talking, they carefully peeked around a tree. Sammy was scared. Would the people be mad at them for being in their back yard? Would they yell at them or worse?

Etta Jean started to run but her shoe fell off and she had to sit down and try to get it on again.

Sammy's eyes were wide and his mouth was open. He was sure they were going to be caught and then what would happen? Sammy crouched behind a tree and Etta Jean huddled close to him. He was scared. Would somebody take him to jail now because he stole the perfume, candy, and flashlight?

—

Chapter Seventeen Thursday - Afternoon and Evening

"Look how those roses are blooming! Aren't they beautiful?" the pretty woman said looking at colorful flowers." She wore dark glasses.

"They are doing well. Maybe that new fertilizer I put on them helped," the handsome, man with a neat beard said. "You've got a real green thumb," he smiled as he looked around the yard.

Sammy and Etta Jean stayed quiet as they huddled behind the tree.

"Well, if we're going to get an early start to the boat in the morning, we better get going," the man said.

"Yes. We have to go to the bank, the cleaners, and the grocery store," the woman said. "I'll get my purse." She started toward the house.

"Boys. Boys, come here a minute."

A tall blond boy came out of the house followed by a younger boy.

"We're going to get food for our long week-end at the boat. You boys clean your rooms. Behave, guys." He patted the older boy's shoulder and rubbed the younger boy's darker hair. The couple went in the small back door of the garage, and soon Sammy heard a car start and back out of the driveway.

The younger boy had a stick and ran around the yard hitting at limbs on trees. He dashed in behind the evergreen tree then stopped suddenly and stared when he saw Sammy and Etta Jean.

"Hi." he said. "Where did you kids come from?"

Sammy and Etta Jean were too scared to say anything. They just stared at the boy.

"Paul. Paul. Come here. There are two kids back here. I don't know who they are."

Paul came hurrying back. He looked shocked to see them. "Well. Who are you and how did you get here?"

"I'm yost and her house burned, and we're hungry, and we don't know how to get to my house, and we don't know where to sleep when it gets dark, and I'm tired," Sammy said with a rush. "And I have to go to the bathroom."

"I thought I heard someone crying while ago. I was upstairs and looked out the window but didn't see anything? Was she crying?" Paul asked Sammy.

"Yeah, she was. She's hungry and I'm hungry, too." Sammy looked anxiously at Etta Jean's red nose and eyes.

"We can get them something to eat, can't we, Paul?" asked the younger boy as he hopped around them. "I'm Bertie. What's your names?"

"She's Etta Jean and I'm Sammy. Can I go to the bathroom?"

Sammy saw Paul wait a minute before answering. "I guess so."

The boys let them through the sliding patio door and into a kitchen. When Paul pointed to a half bath, Sammy rushed in. After he came out Etta Jean used the bathroom.

"Sit down at the table. I'll get you something to eat," Bertie smiled as he went to the refrigerator and cabinets and brought them a package of crackers and a large package of cheese. "Here, Paul, you slice the cheese," the younger boy said.

When Paul sliced off pieces of cheese, Sammy grabbed it and stuffed it in his mouth. Then he asked, "Could I have something to drink? I'm awful thirsty and so is Etta Jean."

Etta Jean slowly ate her cheese and crackers as though she was savoring every bit, while Sammy continued to eat fast. Paul poured them each a glass of cold milk and they both drank. He smiled showing braces on his teeth.

"So good," Etta Jean said. "So good." The children emptied their glasses of cold milk and ate the crackers and cheese quickly.

Etta Jean looked around. "So pretty. Such a pretty house."

Sammy glanced around at the blue and yellow wallpaper, cream ceramic tile floor, and shiny wooden cabinets and cream colored cabinet tops. A green ivy plant in a yellow pot was on the window cell. Sammy thought it looked like most houses he'd been in. Nothing special.

"I'll pour you another glass of milk," the younger boy, who had Band-Aids on both hands, said. He brought over the milk carton. "You pour, Paul. I might spill it."

Sammy thought the milk was the best he ever had. He quickly drank half a glass more and watched Etta Jean drain hers.

"So you're lost?" Paul asked.

Sammy, with a milk mustache, said, "I yive at 867 Yager Street and I got yost. Etta Jean's dad and mom died and her grandma's house burned and they took her to a place. Etta Jean's stepfather didn't want her and she ran away, and she's been yiving in a box but men took it away."

"Wow," Paul said. "Is that right, Etta Jean?" he looked at her.

Sammy saw her nod, then she looked down, and her face got red. He knew she was ashamed to not have a home. He felt like hugging her, but didn't.

Bertie hurried around and brought them each forks and big pieces of chocolate pie on pretty plates. Sammy saw Etta Jean look up and give him a grateful look. Both rushed to take a bite.

"Oh, this is so good," Etta Jean whispered. "Really good," she kept saying between bites. "Thank you, Bertie. Thank you, Paul."

Sammy got his pie eaten before she did as she enjoyed every bite.

"You two were hungry!" Paul said smiling and showing his braces on his teeth again. "Now how can we help you?"

"Call my mommy and daddy. Right now!" Sammy got out of his chair and followed Paul to the telephone where he gave him the number. Paul called it five times but there was no answer.

Sammy's lower lip quivered. "It's gonna be my bertday and I wanta get home."

"I'll call later, Sammy. Don't worry. We'll get you home," Paul smiled at him. "Now what do you two want to do? Our parents aren't here now and you can stay for a while"

"Could I take a bath?" Etta Jean asked. "Then could I maybe wash my clothes? I like to be clean."

Paul sniffed. "I think you both need baths. Come upstairs."

"Call my mommy and daddy again," Sammy insisted.

Paul dialed but received no answer. "I'll try later. Come on upstairs now."

"Could I have my bath first?" Etta Jean asked. "I feel awful dirty. Oh. I don't have any more clothes to wear." She put her hand to her mouth.

"I'll find you something," Paul said.

"Here." Bertie beat him to it as he rushed to a chest of drawers. He pulled out a pair of knit pajamas with superman on the front and handed them to Etta Jean.

"Thank you, Bertie. Paul, could I maybe wash my hair, too?"

Sammy saw Paul roll his eyes at Bertie, and was glad Etta Jean didn't see.

Paul looked at her hair. "I think that would be a good idea. Come on. I'll show you how to turn on the shower and get you the shampoo."

Sammy followed along.

Etta Jean looked at the blue and white bathroom with its big tub and shower. "So nice," Etta Jean said wistfully. "So pretty."

"After you wash your hair, you can use Mom's hairbrush," Paul said as he and Sammy left the bathroom.

"Come in my room, Sammy," Bertie called. "I'll show you my new remote control fire engine." He peeled off a Band-Aid. His thumb only had a scratch.

Sammy liked the fire engine and soon Sammy and Bertie were on the floor playing with the truck and cars while Paul watched them.

Etta Jean came out of the bathroom brushing her hair and wearing the superman pajamas. She had her dirty clothes rolled in a tight bundle and carried her backpack.

"Your turn to take a bath, Sammy," Paul said. "I'll help you."

"Here, Etta Jean, you can have a pair of my socks," Bertie said.

"I'll just wear them until mine get washed and dried. Thank you," she whispered and pulled them on. "Socks with no holes in them! Thanks!" she said as the boys laughed.

Paul helped Sammy bathe and wash his hair. Then he got him Bertie's long sweatshirt and underpants for him to wear. Sammy did feel better after he was clean. Generous Bertie gave Sammy some socks, too.

Sammy handed his soiled clothes to Etta Jean who was trying to get enough string to tie her shoe.

"Those shoes are all worn out. Paul, throw those awful shoes of Etta Jean's in the trash. She can have mine." Bertie said as he handed her a pair of Reeboks that were in good condition. "I don't wear these shoes anymore 'cause they hurt my feet. You take them," Bertie insisted.

"Well," Etta Jean took the shoes and looked them over. "If you don't wear them— they're 100 times better than my old shoes. At least that," she said as she gave Bertie a beaming smile. She put on the shoes and stood up. "They fit me just fine. They're great. Thank you, Bertie." She walked around the room then stopped and looked at

Paul. "Now can I wash our clothes? I could wash them in the bathtub."

"Naw. We'll put them in the washer." Paul bent down to pick up the soiled clothing, sniffed, then said, "You carry them down, Etta Jean."

"Could I wash the blanket, too?" She pulled the old blanket out of her backpack.

Sammy saw Paul nod and pick up the blanket. They left the room.

"Wait," Sammy said. "Wait." He hurried after them, took his jeans from Etta Jean, went through his jeans pocket and took out the graph and pencil. He started to show the graph to Bertie but dropped it. "Oh, Clinker Dab!" he said as he picked it up.

"What did you say?" Paul asked.

"He says 'Clinker Dab' all the time," Etta Jean told the boys and giggled. They laughed with her.

"Why do you say that, Sammy?" Paul questioned.

"Well, one time I fell down and said a bad word that I can't tell you. My mommy told me to never say that again or she would wash out my mouth with soap. We went to a park and they had little chunks they called clinkers on the path, and I thought it was a neat word."

157

"Yeah, neat," Bertie said thoughtfully.

They all walked downstairs and watched Paul turn on the washer and put in soap. "I'll throw those old socks and shoes of yours in the trash, Etta Jean. They're nothing but holes."

"All right. I'd pay for my new shoes and socks if I could, Paul."

"Naw. Forget it." Sammy saw Paul look embarrassed.

They all went back to Bertie's room where Sammy laid his graph and pencil on the dresser. Bertie had a dish of jellybeans for them.

"Real candy. I haven't had that for a long, long time," Etta Jean beamed as she sucked on a red jellybean. "So good."

Now that Sammy was in a house, clean, and full of food, he became a clown. He made faces, smirked, and rolled his eyes as he ate his candy. He noticed for the first time that Etta Jean's wavy hair was smooth and neat. He pretended to brush his hair rolling his eyes as he did so.

Etta Jean tried to tie back her hair with the dirty, twisted ribbon. Sammy saw Bertie watch her, then run out and back again with a small length of white package ribbon, which Etta Jean accepted gratefully. She threw the yellow ribbon in his wastebasket and tied back her hair with the new ribbon.

"Bertie, you give me so much." She smiled and Bertie grinned.

"Sammy, how long have you been lost and where have you been?" Paul asked.

Sammy told them about not telling the truth to his parents and staying to play in the tent.

"Where did you sleep when you were lost?" Bertie asked.

Sammy told them about sleeping in the trucks then about eating the teenager's cheese burger. "One truck driver said awful bad words." His eyes were round with shock. I can't tell you the words. They're a-w-f-u-l." He dragged out the word while the others laughed. "He was mean so I put pickle juice in his thermos and he drank it and said more bad words."

"You put pickle juice in his thermos?" Paul laughed showing his braces, and Bertie laughed and laughed and Etta Jean laughed her deep, throaty laugh. Then the boys laughed more when they heard her.

"And a heavy woman had ripped pants and her underpants showed." Everyone laughed at his story and especially when he told how the skinny girl hit him and he hit her, then she chased him, and he tried to spit on her shoes.

159

Paul wanted to hear more of his adventures.

Sammy told how he scared the girl looking at fur coats and the others laughed. "It was awful spooky in the department store at night. I heard strange sounds and I thought a monster bigger than three wheel barrels was going to grab my neck." He rolled his eyes as he talked and Bertie laughed so hard, he lay down on the floor holding his stomach.

Sammy loved the attention so told them about throwing the board in the cow pie and getting manure all over Perfect Prissy Sibyl. He giggled when he whispered that he had pinched Minnie Mouse's behind at Disney World. They all laughed and laughed. Bertie laughed so hard he rolled back and forth.

"Tell us some more about Perfect Prissy Sybil," Paul urged.

"Well." Sammy thought a moment. "One time she made a hole in the bottom of my grape juice carton and I dribbled juice all over my clean white shirt. She yaughed at me and said I dumb." He smacked his hands together. "But I got even with her. We were staying at her house and I sneaked a glass of milk in the bathroom and put it in her shampoo bottle."

The other three laughed more. "Then what happened?"

"Well, my Aunt Bertha tried to wash her hair, and she told Mom that she got a bad bottle of shampoo. Nobody knew I did it."

Sammy moved across the room and sat on the lower bunk bed. "Sibyl's mean. She told me a tiger was under my bed and I got scared and cried for Mommy and she said I was a silly 'M-a-m-a's boy.' I'm not. She pushed me off my bike yots of times and when I cried, she told her mother—who always believes her—that I was just clumsy." He gave a big sigh. "But I'd even kinda yike to see ole Sibyl again. Can I call Mommy now?"

"Sure." Paul took him into his parent's bedroom where Sammy dialed his telephone number three times, but there was no answer. They returned to the bedroom after Paul put the clothes into the dryer.

Sitting again on the floor in Bertie's room they talked and talked. Paul showed them a little doll that was his grandmother's.

Etta Jean told about Hank and Kate and how Kate walked and they all laughed some more. Sammy was pleased to see Etta Jean act so happy after she'd been sad all morning. They even laughed at Etta Jean's description of how she managed to cook potatoes and onions for her grandmother.

Bertie told how Paul slipped at the bus stop and accidentally knocked down a little boy Sammy's age, and how the small boy got up and hit him. They all thought it hilariously funny, even Paul.

When Sammy told them he wanted Etta Jean to be his sister, everyone was quiet, and Sammy saw the sad look on Etta Jean's face.

After a while Etta Jean asked, "Are you going to clean up your rooms like your Dad said?"

"Oh, prunes!" Paul said it like it was a real naughty word and they all laughed some more.

"I'll help," Etta Jean said. She straightened Bertie's bed, and picked up dirty clothes and put them in the clothes hamper. She straightened his books. Paul and Sammy ran into Paul's room where Sammy helped him. When Paul heard the buzzer of the dryer, he and Sammy ran downstairs, got the clothes, and carried them up.

Etta Jean looked at them then at Paul. "I guess we'd better put on our own clothes on and leave," she said sadly.

"Let's have them stay all night. We'll hide them in my room, so Mom won't know. Come on, Paul, let's do it," Bertie begged.

Paul thought a moment then smiled. "OK." He laughed. "That'll be cool. Etta Jean can sleep on the top bunk in here and Sammy in the bottom one. Bertie can sleep in my room."

"Well, I wanta go home," Sammy protested.

"It's getting late. I don't think your folks will be home until later tonight. You can call your parents in the morning. They'll come get you."

Sammy chuckled. It would be fun staying with Paul and Bertie tonight. "All right," he said while Etta Jean beamed.

Suddenly they heard the garage door go up. "I'll put your clothes, blanket, and backpack on this shelf in the closet, and you can put them on in the morning. Put the stuff you're wearing in the clothes hamper when you change. Now you better hide in the closet, kids," Paul whispered. "Don't say a word, Bertie. We'll bring up some food later."

He turned as he went out the door. "Now be quiet. Dad and Mom might be mad if they find you here." He smiled showing his shiny braces. "I think it's cool that you're staying."

Etta Jean and Sammy went into the closet and sat down on the floor. She kept reaching up and looking at Bertie's shirts, jeans, and

163

sweaters that were hanging above her. Cars, books, and other toys were on the floor of the closet and she picked each one up and looked it over. "Bertie has so many clothes and toys. I never saw so many," Etta Jean whispered. "Oh, there's a red shirt just like the one you were wearing when I saw you Saturday."

Sammy reached up and pulled the shirt nearer. "Yeah, it's just like mine. I got black stuff from the fire on it," he told her.

"So many clothes and toys," Etta Jean murmured.

"Oh, I have more stuff than this," Sammy bragged as he played with a Game Boy. He showed it to Etta Jean and taught her to play.

Later, Paul brought up a plastic bowl with roast beef, mashed potatoes and gravy, rolls, peas, carrot sticks and an oatmeal cookie for each. Bertie carried up two paper plates, two forks, and a spoon.

Paul took a spoon and divided the food evenly between the two paper plates and handed them to the Etta Jean and Sammy. They both ate it all, then Paul sent them separately to the bathroom and told them to drink water out of paper cups that were in a little container that hung on the wall.

Back in the bedroom, Etta Jean, Sammy, and Bertie sat on the floor of Bertie's room again while Paul sat on the lower bunk.

"Can you call my parents again tonight, Paul?" Sammy asked.

"No, I can't. If I did, Dad would know you were hiding here and maybe make you leave. You can call in the morning."

"I got an good idea," Bertie rushed across the room. "I'll give you money to call a taxi and you can go home and surprise your folks." He grabbed a bank shaped like a mushroom and opened it. He handed Etta Jean eight-dollar bills and some change. "Won't it be fun to s'prise your mom and dad, Sammy?"

"Yeah." Sammy's face lit up and he raised his shoulders with eyes sparkling. Then he noticed Etta Jean looking at the floor. He could not see her face but knew she looked sad.

"Dad'll be mad at you for giving your money away, Bertie," Paul said.

"Big deal," Bertie shrugged it off. "Granddad will give me more money when I see him and Dad won't know."

"My daddy will come and pay you back, Bertie. Soon as I get home," Sammy said

"Well, OK." Paul agreed. "Etta Jean, that should be enough to get you to Yager Street. I'll write down our telephone number and you kids call and ask to speak to me so I'll know you're all right."

165

"Don't ask to talk to him. Ask to talk to me," Bertie stood in front of Etta Jean.

"Sammy will call," Etta Jean whispered.

"You can. You'll be there. You're my new sister," Sammy said.

Paul wiggled a foot. "Etta Jean, uh," he spoke slowly, "uh, Sammy's parents might not, uh, uh, be able to have you stay." His voice was kind. "Don't be disappointed if they don't."

"I know," Etta Jean looked down.

"Listen, my uncle's a social worker. He'll find you a place to live. Just call here, and I'll get him to help you."

Etta Jean nodded.

"He'll just sent her back to her stepdad who doesn't want her," Sammy said. "My folks'll want her."

"Well, I hope so," Paul's voice did not sound encouraging. "Remember what I said, Etta Jean. My uncle'll help you. Bertie, we better go downstairs. Dad or Mom might come up and wonder what we're doing. You kids hide in the closet again until we come back up."

The children went back into the closet. Sammy watched Etta Jean pick up each toy again and look it over. He was tired and leaned over against a big stuffed gorilla and dozed.

After about two hours the boys came back upstairs and Etta Jean and Sammy used the bathroom again. Paul told them to go back into the closet until his mother came in and kissed Bertie good-night.

After Bertie went to the bathroom and put on his pajamas, he came back and crawled in the lower bunk.

Sammy peeked through a crack in the door and saw Bertie's mother come in, pull the blanket higher on his chest, and kiss him. Sammy heard her whisper, "Love you." It made him long for his mother. He saw some tears on Etta Jean's cheeks.

Bertie waited a while, then opened the closet door and motioned them to quietly come out. Paul came in and whispered, "Kids, in the morning wait 'till we leave, then go downstairs and eat. There's ham in the bottom drawer of the refrigerator and bread in that breadbox on top of the counter. I left you some cookies in there, too. Grapes are in the refrigerator. There's milk and orange juice. Fix yourselves breakfast."

"Oh, thanks, Paul. Uh... Paul, can we take grapes and cookies with us?' Etta Jean whispered.

Sammy interrupted, "We won't need to take any stuff, Etta Jean. We'll eat at my house."

Paul looked at Etta Jean and nodded. "Take what you need. Fix ham sandwiches and take some soda pop," he said. "Also take cookies or whatever."

"Thank you, thank you, thank you," Etta Jean answered as the boys left the room. She quietly climbed into the top bunk.

Sammy got into the lower. "It's good to sleep in a bed," Sammy whispered.

"So good. To be warm and not be scared and in a soft bed. So good," she whispered back. "So good."

Where will Etta Jean go after I get home, Sammy worried. Where will she sleep? How will she get to go to school?

—

Chapter Eighteen - Friday Morning

"Etta Jean, Etta Jean, wake up," Sammy heard Paul whisper. "We're going to our boat now. Sammy, are you awake? Good. You kids be careful. I told you about stuff to eat and take what food you want. Stay in bed 'till you hear us leave." He looked nervously out the bedroom door.

"Paul, can I take another bath?" Etta Jean asked.

"Sure, you can," Paul nodded as he came back into the room. "Don't leave things around that Mom can find, or she'll know you've been here. Go out the front door and check it twice to make sure it's locked. Here's our 'phone number and the number to call the taxi on this paper. I'll put it on the dresser. Be sure to call us."

"Thank you, thank you, Paul. Thank you for the shoes and socks and washing our clothes and letting us take baths and sleep here. Thanks for letting us have fun yesterday afternoon."

"Yeah." Paul put his finger to his lips and left just as Bertie slipped into the room. "Bye, Sammy and Etta Jean. Glad you stayed here. Having you kids here was the most fun I ever had," he said in a low voice his eyes twinkling. "Come back again," he waved as he left.

"Wasn't the most fun I ever had," Sammy complained. "I wanta go home."

"You will. Today," Etta Jean told him as she turned over and snuggled deeper under the blanket.

Sammy looked around the unfamiliar room with its cream walls and a bright border of cars around the ceiling. Tomorrow he would be home and see his Sesame Street figures on the walls.

"Get up, Etta Jean. We gotta go."

"We can't 'til they leave, Sammy." Etta Jean's voice sounded sleepy.

Sammy waited and waited listening for the car to leave. He was still tired from all his walking and, as he waited, he went back to sleep.

Some time later Sammy woke up. He listened for a while but didn't hear anyone downstairs. He crawled out of bed and stood on the lower bunk where he could see Etta Jean. She slept. One arm was stretched above her head and her hair spread over her pillow. He watched her for a while and thought how nice it was to see her resting in a real bed. He knew she had had little rest since her grandmother's house burned.

Watching her a little while longer, he couldn't wait another minute. "Etta Jean. Etta Jean. Wake up. We get to go home today."

Etta Jean opened her eyes then closed them. She stretched and smiled then stretched again. "O.K. Sammy. You go to the bathroom first. Wash good."

Sammy got his clothes off the shelf and dressed. Etta Jean came downstairs still wearing Bertie's pajamas. The children were quiet although they knew the family had gone. Sammy found bread and helped to make toast. Etta Jean took ham out of the refrigerator, and the children made ham and toast sandwiches. Etta Jean was afraid to pour orange juice because the container was too full and she didn't want to spill it, but she poured two tall glasses of milk.

"Yet's go. Yet's call the taxi and go. I want to see Mommy and Daddy," Sammy hopped around the room.

"Eat more toast and ham, Sammy. Yesterday you kept pulling up your jeans 'cause they're so loose."

"I'm eating as much as I can," Sammy whined. He watched Etta Jean as she carefully washed their dishes, dried them, and placed them in the cabinet.

Then she walked through the living room and dining room admiring the furniture and pictures, picking up little objects, and talking about how pretty they were, as she carefully replaced them. "I never saw such a pretty house," she said quietly.

"Our house is pretty," Sammy told her. "I told you you'd have your own room. There's not much furniture in that room because Mommy was going to buy it when she knew she would get a baby."

"Your mom wants a baby. She won't want me."

"Yes, she will. Tomorrow's my bertday and all I want is a sister and I've got you." He smiled at Etta and she smiled at him.

"Sammy, don't talk about it. Not anymore!" Etta Jean was firm.

"I'm gonna call my parents right now." Sammy dialed his telephone number three times, but the line was busy. Maybe his mother was talking to his grandmother. Sammy was disgusted and impatient when Etta Jean said she was going to take another bath. He went back to Bertie's bedroom and played with the Game Boy.

"Lt. Sloan, have you heard anything at all?" Larry asked with a sad voice. This made at least the twelfth time he had telephoned Lt. Sloan this week.

"Sorry, Mr. Hendricks. Some of our men thought they might have seen your son yesterday walking down a sidewalk with a girl older than he is. They circled the block several times, but the children disappeared. We're doing the best we can and following every lead."

"Well, thanks," Larry said turning sadly to Emily as he hung up the 'phone.

Emily was holding the soiled red shirt up to her face. She was never far from it as it comforted her as much as anything could. She walked across the room and pulled up her slacks, which were too loose.

"You're losing weight, Emily."

"Yes. A little. I'll gain it back when Sammy comes home."

He watched Emily hold the red shirt. "Are you going to wash that, Emily?"

She shrugged her shoulders. Larry knew the shrug meant if Sammy came home. Larry sadly faced reality. He knew that every day that passed made it less likely for Sammy to ever return.

Sammy took the graph and pencil from the dresser, and marked an X under F. "Only one more day till my bertday," he said quietly putting them back in his pocket. He played with Bertie's remote control fire engine.

Etta Jean came out of the bathroom, dressed in her old green sweat suit, which now looked clean but still ragged. He noticed she had washed her hair again, brushed it smooth, and tied it back with the white gift ribbon Bertie had given her.

"You washed your hair again, Etta Jean," he whimpered.

"I want to look as good as I can when we get to your parent's house." She tried to smooth her ragged sweatshirt.

Sammy followed her back to the bathroom. She put the clothes they had worn in the clothes hamper. With a clean washcloth, she tried to wash her teeth. "I wish my toothbrush hadn't burned up," she said.

"I'll see that you get one," Sammy said and watched her as she wiped out the tub and sink and hung the bath towels straight on the towel racks.

Back In the bedroom she tried to make the upper bunk neatly, crawling around over it as she did so. It was easier to make the bottom bunk.

Sammy followed her from room to room. "You yook real purty, Etta Jean. Now come on. Yet's go. We slept a yong time and it's almost 10:00 o'clock now. Come on." Sammy was hopping around.

"It's 'look' instead of 'yook,' and 'let's' instead of 'yet's, and 'long' instead of 'yong,' Sammy."

"Yeah. Sure. Come on!"

"OK. We can take some food. Paul said we could." Etta Jean reached for her blanket, checked her backpack to make sure her piece of comb, picture, flashlight, and perfume were in it, then folded the blanket and shoved it inside. She took the scrap of paper with telephone numbers on it and put it in her pocket. Sammy hurried her downstairs to the kitchen and watched while she made ham sandwiches. Finding plastic bags she carefully wrapped the sandwiches and put them in a larger bag. She rinsed grapes and counted out six small cookies that she wrapped. At the last moment she took two cans of soda from the refrigerator.

Sammy tried twice to call his parents but the line was still busy. He took out his graph and made a mark for Friday.

"Sammy, you have to carry the soda," she said putting the cans in a small paper bag. "My backpack will be too full." Before putting the food in her backpack, she took out the picture of herself and her mother and kissed it. After she packed the food was in her worn backpack, it was quite bulky.

Sammy watched her and was going to say something about her kissing a picture, but remembered how she felt sad when he said something about it before. He took the sack. "Come on. I wanta go."

"I sure like the presents you gave me," she whispered.

"Mommy and Daddy will give you more," he told her strutting around the room.

Etta Jean looked sad and struggled into the straps of her shabby backpack. She looked around the kitchen. "It's so pretty," she said.

"Don't know why you're taking those sandwiches. We're gonna be home," Sammy told her.

Etta Jean walked into the living room and Sammy followed. "Everything is so beautiful in this house. It must be wonderful to live in a nice house like this."

"You will, Etta Jean. You'll yike our house."

Etta Jean looked at him and shook her head. "I wish it could be like that, Sammy. I prayed last night. But I know your folks will tell me they don't want me—just like Mrs. Lyons did. I told you not to talk about it anymore."

Sammy walked over and took her hand. "My parents will want you."

Etta Jean was quiet. "Would you really, really, really think your parents would want me, Sammy?"

"Sure, they will." Sammy said, but now he wasn't sure. He walked to the front door.

Etta Jean telephoned for a taxi using the number from the scrap of paper Paul had given her. As they left she made sure and checked twice that the front door was locked. They waited outside.

"Look, Sammy, how nice my new shoes and socks look. They're not worn out. My socks don't have any holes at all. Look how nice my shoes tie with those long shoe strings."

Sammy knelt beside Etta Jean and felt her toes. "These shoes are too yong for you. They're too big."

177

Etta Jean jerked away. "They are not," she said in a strangely cross voice. "They fit me fine." She walked away from him.

Soon the cab came and the children climbed in the back seat.

"To 867 Yager Street," Sammy said and beamed at Etta Jean. "I'm going home," he said and his eyes were wide and happy.

Etta Jean took his hand. "Sammy, I really liked being with you. You made it so it wasn't so lonesome."

"I won't forget you, 'cause you'll be my...si...... I hope," he said wistfully. He took a deep breath. "I yike playing with you 'cause you yaugh and you're fun."

"Talk plain, Sammy. It's 'like' and 'laugh.' You say everything else good."

"Yeah. Sure." Sammy bounced on the seat.

"It was fun talking with you. I told you kids at school don't talk or play with me much. You've been the nicest kid I've been around since Angela was so nice."

"Kids should play with you."

"Well, I don't dress right or look right." She sighed. "Here's the paper with Paul and Bertie's phone number. You call them."

"No, you call them, Etta Jean. You keep it."

"Sammy, take it." Etta Jean laid the scrap of paper on the seat between them and looked out the window.

Sammy picked the scrap of paper and stuffed it in his jean pocket.

Soon the cab pulled into a driveway. "Here we are," the driver said reaching back for Etta Jean to put money in his hand.

"This isn't Mommy and Daddy's house," Sammy wailed. "Take us to Mommy and Daddy's house."

"Listen, kids. This is 867 Yager Street like you told me. Now hop out."

Etta Jean paid the driver and she and Sammy got out of the cab.

"We'll go to the door anyway," Etta Jean said. She was also very disappointed and tried to hide this from Sammy, who was about to cry.

An older, balding man dressed all in brown opened the door.

"Is this 867 Yager Street?" Etta Jean asked.

"Yes, it is. What can I do for you?"

"Do you know Sammy?" Etta Jean pushed Sammy forward.

"No, I don't believe I do. He's a handsome boy and if I had seen him before, I would remember that red hair."

"My Mommy and Daddy are s'posed to yive at 867 Yager Street. Where's my mommy and daddy?" Sammy demanded.

"Does this house look like the house where your mother and father live?"

"No. It's not my house," Sammy said sadly and turned away.

"Thank you," Etta Jean said and the two children trudged down the sidewalk. "Maybe you got the numbers wrong and your house is really close."

"I didn't get the numbers wrong, Etta Jean." Sammy's shoulders were sagging and tears rolled down his cheeks. "I'll never get home. I'll never see my mommy and daddy again."

"Yes, you will, Sammy." Etta Jean put her arm around Sammy's shoulders. "We'll find them. They must live just a few houses away. We'll walk 'till we find them. This is Yager Street—they must be on down this way."

"I don't know where I yive now." Sammy bit his lip to keep from crying. "I'll never get home. Tomorrow's my bertday and I won't be home."

—

Chapter Nineteen - Friday Afternoon And Evening

They walked up and down Yager Street, then moved over to the next street and the next street and walked some more. After a couple of hours, they sat on a curb and ate the ham sandwiches. Sammy complained he was thirsty, so they shared one of the sodas.

After walking quite a while longer and looking and looking for Sammy's house they found a little park and wearily sat on a park bench.

"Can we have some cookies?" Sammy asked.

"All right," Etta Jean dug in her backpack and found the small plastic bag with the cookies. The six oatmeal raisin cookies were a little crumbled, but Sammy didn't care. Etta Jean would only let him have one and also ate just one. He ate his very quickly.

After using the bathrooms, they stretched out on separate park benches, and slept a little. When they woke up, the sky was cloudy. Etta Jean insisted that they go to the bathrooms again. They each drank twice from the water fountain before then walked on.

"It looks like it's gonna rain, Etta Jean." Sammy rubbed his eyes. "I'm scared of thunder and lightning." He looked at the sky.

"I don't like it either." Sammy saw Etta Jean keep looking up at the clouds. They continued walking and Sammy watched the swirling clouds.

Suddenly there was a crack of thunder and a flash of lightning. Sammy and Etta Jean grabbed each other. Then it started to rain and the children ran. Etta Jean spotted a big, dark blue Cadillac in an open garage.

"Come on." She grabbed Sammy's hand and they dashed up the driveway and into the garage. Opening the door to the back seat she pushed Sammy in and climbed in after him.

"If anyone comes out, get down on the floor fast, Sammy."

"Yeah. Sure. What if someone comes out and gets in the back seat?"

Etta Jean laughed her deep throated laugh. "They'll be surprised!" She laughed some more. "They probably won't and we have a place to keep dry and sleep tonight."

The thunder crashed, and lightning flashed. The rain came down hard. "I'm sure glad we don't have to be in the rain," Etta Jean said. "You wouldn't be much help in keeping us dry."

Sammy laughed a little, then leaned over against the door, listened to the rain, and dozed.

Etta Jean was tired, too. She took off her backpack, tucked one strap over her arm, stretched her other arm out toward Sammy, and slept.

They slept quite a long time when they were awakened by voices.

"Hurry up. We're going to be late, Shirley," the tall man said.

"I'll just get the snacks, Bill," the woman answered.

"Looks like the rain has stopped. We needed it," the man said as he walked toward the car.

Etta Jean grabbed Sammy and they slid to the floor. Sammy's eyes and mouth were round and he was frightened again.

The couple got into the car and the pretty woman put a large tray of food on the seat between them. Sammy gave a sigh of relief that nobody was getting into the back seat and smiled at Etta Jean who smiled back.

As the man drove, the couple talked about streets that were closed for repairs and how they had to take different streets. When they watched for street signs, Sammy quietly slid his hand up over the arm rest, carefully pulled back the plastic wrap, and brought back a small handful of celery stuffed with peanut butter. He handed the food to Etta Jean who was having a difficult time keeping from laughing as he reached for another handful. Some of the celery this time was stuffed with cream cheese. He reached for a third handful, then replaced the plastic wrap.

Soon the couple arrived at their friends' house. The woman picked up the tray, looked at it, frowned a little, then moved the pieces so they filled up the tray. They got out and hurried up the sidewalk.

Sammy took a bite of celery with peanut butter and he and Etta Jean giggled at the crunching sound in the closed car. Etta Jean crunched hers and they laughed and laughed. Sammy thought again how much fun Etta Jean was.

"So good. So good," Etta Jean kept saying as she ate more.

"You say everything is so good, Etta Jean. 'So good.' 'So good,'" he mocked her.

Etta Jean's feelings were hurt. "Well, maybe you had better food than I had." She put her head down and sniffled. "It's bad when you make fun of people by mocking them. I don't like it." She looked down.

"I'm sorry." Sammy tried to take her hand but she pulled away. "Someday you'll have good things to eat every day."

Etta Jean raised her head and looked at him. "Oh, I hope so."

They ate the grapes then Etta Jean would only allow them to eat one cookie each and saved the other two cookies.

Sammy wanted both cookies then, but knew better than argue with Etta Jean. He tugged and opened the last soda and they took turns drinking from it. Sammy burped loud and Etta Jean laughed. He managed to burp again, because he liked to hear her laugh. She pulled the ragged blanket from the backpack and carefully covered Sammy and then pulled some over herself.

"Your blanket smells better tonight," Sammy whispered.

"Yes, it does. I like to be clean," Etta Jean said. She turned her head to one side and settled back onto the seat and soon went to sleep. Sammy watched the moving clouds out the car window, then he slept, too.

He woke up when he heard car doors slamming. Peeking out, he saw the couple coming to the car. "Etta Jean. They're coming. Get on the floor."

They barely had time to crouch down when the woman opened the back door and threw her white coat on the seat without looking into the car.

The scared children looked at each other and tried not to giggle.

"Which street should we taking home?" her husband Bill asked.

"Whatever. Barbara had a blouse just like mine," Shirley said.

"I know," Bill answered. "Gene and I thought you both looked nice."

It started raining again as they drove and the windshield wipers swished back and forth. When they pulled into the garage, the woman reached in the back seat, and Etta Jean picked up the coat and handed it to her. She took it without noticing as Etta Jean and Sammy covered their mouths so they wouldn't laugh out loud. The couple went into the house. Soon the overhead light in the garage went out and it was very dark.

"I'm scared," Sammy whispered.

"Don't be. I'm right here." Etta Jean got the flashlight out of the backpack, turned it on, and looked around the garage. "I'm sure glad you had this flashlight, and gave it to me," she told him. "I like it a lot."

She flashed the light around the garage again, got out of the car, and put the empty soda can and plastic bags in a trash can. She looked around some more and saw a yellow golf jacket laying over a golf bag. She got it and got back in the back seat.

"Sammy, you crawl in the front seat and cover up with the blanket. I'll cover up with this jacket."

"How you gonna do that?"

Etta Jean handed him the flashlight then put her legs into the sleeves of the jacket and pulled the rest up as high as it would go. She laughed. Sammy giggled and giggled seeing how silly she looked. He lay back down, then sat up, took off his jacket and handed it back to her.

"Thanks, Sammy." She pulled it up to her chin and snuggled down.

Sammy lay back down. "Etta Jean. Let's pray that you're my sister for sure."

187

"I told you I prayed that my mother would get well and that my grandma would quit forgetting. I guess I don't know how to pray or God doesn't hear me."

"God hears your prayers, Etta Jean. You pray now. I'm gonna." Sammy closed his eyes and folded his hands. "Please, God, yet Etta Jean be my sister. And please get me home to Mommy and Daddy for my bertday." He stretched. Hearing a noise from the backseat, he looked back in the dim light and saw Etta Jean on her knees with her head bowed and her hands folded.

Tears came to Sammy's eyes. "Please, God, answer her prayer," he whispered softly. Turning off the flashlight, he thought about his own bed and his mother and father. He heard it start to rain again. He wiggled around on the front seat trying to be comfortable and his backside hit the steering wheel.

With Sammy's soiled shirt on the pillow between them, Emily folded her hands and prayed, "Dear Lord, Sammy's been gone so long. Please keep him safe and warm tonight and let him sleep and be comforted. Please let him be dry and not out in this storm. Please bring precious Sammy home to us. Amen."

She *kept her hands folded. Tomorrow's Sammy's birthday. Will he ever be home? Where is he tonight? Was he out in the rain? How will he get home tomorrow?*

—

Chapter 20 - Saturday Morning

"Wake up, Sammy. We better leave." Sammy felt Etta Jean pat his arm as she reached between the car seats.

Sammy tried to wipe the "duck dobby," from his eyes. That is what Etta Jean said her grandmother called eye matter. He sleepily looked around. Daylight came in through the glass of the side door of the garage. He looked at the dashboard near him as he lay on the front seat, then remembered he had slept in a car. Sitting up, he yawned, and handed the bunched up blanket over the seat to Etta Jean.

He heard her chuckle as she wiggled out of the golf jacket, then folded the blanket and put it in her backpack. She slid out of the car, brushed some crumbs out of the back seat, and hung the golf jacket where she found it.

"Come on," she whispered. "Close the car door quietly." They slipped out the garage side door. Once again they started walking down the sidewalk.

"I was thinking. Your mom and dad must live real close. Let's find that house at 867 Yager house again and talk to that man."

"Yeah. Sure," Sammy said wearily as he walked a step behind Etta Jean. They walked about an hour but didn't find the man's house.

Sammy was tired of walking. "You promised you'd take me home. Why don't you do it?" he kicked Etta Jean's leg.

She turned around, surprised. "You kicked me! You're mean." She kicked his leg. "I'm doing the best I can!"

"Well, it ain't good enough. I ain't home," Sammy kicked her again.

Etta Jean kicked him and they exchanged kicks until Etta Jean fell on the grass and started laughing. Sammy sprawled beside her and laughed, too.

Sammy frowned. "I'm sorry I was mean," he touched her torn sleeve.

"Oh Sammy, you're funny and nice." Etta Jean took his hand.

"Nice? Even when I kick you?"

"No, not then, but most times," Etta Jean giggled some more.

The children got up and walked down the street holding hands.

Suddenly Sammy tore his hand away. "I ain't holdin' hands with no girl."

Etta Jean laughed her deep musical laugh and walked on.

Sammy sat down on the grass, reached in his pocket, took out his graph and pencil and made an X for Saturday. "It's my bertday," he whispered as he got to his feet and caught up with Etta Jean.

They looked and looked for his house, but couldn't find it. They walked more and now it was past mid-morning.

"I'm gonna ask that man who's jogging," Etta Jean. "Mister, where is 867 Yager Street?" Sammy saw the skinny man, who was wearing blue running shorts and no shirt, pause for a couple seconds.

"Three blocks that way, two blocks to the right," he pointed than ran on.

"Only five more blocks, Sammy," Etta Jean smiled and patted his arm.

"I'm thirsty," Sammy complained as they started walking down the street again. "And I'm hungry."

"Oh, I saved those two cookies for us." Etta Jean dug in her backpack and pulled them out. Sammy gobbled his down as she ate hers more slowly.

"I'm still hungry," Sammy whined.

"So'm I."

"I'm thirsty."

"So'm I."

"I wanta go home."

Etta Jean had no answer for that.

He understood and touched her hand. She smiled at him as she reached down to pull her socks up. He knew the shoes were too big and were probably hurting her but she didn't complain.

"You've been a good friend, Sammy. Better ever than Angela. I'll miss you so much."

Sammy didn't know what to say. He still hoped his parents would want her, but now he thought they wouldn't, as he knew they wanted a baby girl.

Finally they came to 867 Yager Street.

The balding, man again came to the door. He was dressed in gray. "You children here again? Can't you find your parent's house?"

Sammy shook his head and had trouble holding tears back. "It's my bertday and I wanna go home."

"Well, come on in," the kind man said. "We'll see what we can do."

The man patted Sammy's head and smiled at Etta Jean. "Now tell me again where you live."

"First, could we use your bathroom, please," Etta Jean asked.

"Yes, indeed. Right there," the man pointed down the hall.

"Sammy, wash your face and hands with soap," Etta Jean bossed.

Sammy gave a smirk and then went to the bathroom.

While Etta Jean took her turn, the man asked, "Are you youngsters hungry? Would you like something to eat, son?" he patted Sammy's bright hair again.

Sammy nodded and smiled.

"Tell you what. I'll scramble some eggs, cook some bacon, and fix toast for you. How does that sound?"

Etta Jean was back in the kitchen and heard him. "That sounds good."

After they ate and drank their milk, Etta Jean said, "Thank you. That was so good. So…"

Sammy saw her look at him. I'll never tease her again for saying, 'so good,' he decided. Suddenly he felt a poke in the ribs and she glared at him.

"Ah, thank you for breakfast," he muttered embarrassed.

"Glad I could get you hungry children something to eat. Now let's figure out how to get you home."

Suddenly Sammy felt two years younger. "I wanta go home. I wanta sit on my mommy's yap. My yegs are tired from walking so much."

"Lap. Legs." Sammy saw Etta Jean give him a long look.

"Mister, he says 'y' for 'l' sometimes. Is there a Lager Street, too?"

"Yes," Sammy grinned and jumped up. Yes. I live at Yager Street."

"Mister, I think he lives at 867 Lager Street," Etta Jean said smiling.

"Well, I'd drive you over to Lager Street. It isn't far, but I have a problem. One of our cars is being repaired and my wife has taken the other one to the grocery store. How about if I telephone for a cab?"

"We don't have any money," Sammy felt sorry for Etta Jean when she told the man that. He knew she was embarrassed the way she held her head down.

"No problem," the kind man said. After he telephoned, he said to Etta Jean. "Child, here's $10.00. You give that to the driver and he will give you money back. You give him a dollar and you and the boy keep the rest. Ok?"

"Thanks, Mister," she smiled at him.

"Thanks, Mister," Sammy echoed. He didn't have to wait for Etta Jean's poke that time. "Can we wait outside?"

Sammy was so excited on the ride home that he bounced up and down on the seat. "That's my house," he called as they drove into a driveway. "That's my house. Mommy. Daddy." He jumped from the cab and ran up the sidewalk.

Emily was sitting quietly at the table. A cup half full of coffee was in front of her, and she had a hand on the knit red shirt lying on her lap.

Larry stared at it wondering if he would ever see his precious son again. He heard a car and looked out the window and saw his bright haired son getting out of the taxi. "Emily, I think you'll be washing that red shirt! SAMMY'S HERE!" he shouted and dashed out the door and picked up his small son. Emily was right behind him.

"I'm home!" Sammy hugged his daddy. He was giggling but Larry and Emily were both crying with happiness. As they went into the house, Emily sat down and pulled him onto her lap. He heard her murmuring "Thank you, God," over and over as she held him tight.

196

Tears of joy were rolling down Emily's face and Sammy wiped them away. "Don't cry, Mommy. I'm home!"

He didn't see Etta Jean slowly getting out of the cab.

"Are you all right, son? Are you all right?" his father asked as he wiped his nose and eyes. He knelt by Emily with his hand on Sammy's leg. His mother held him close.

"Course I'm all right. I played in a tent," Sammy bragged. "I rode in a flower truck, but they didn't bring flowers home, then I rode in a big truck all the way almost to Dayton, then I rode in another big truck and the driver talked bad, then Etta Jean took care of me. We stayed in her box house, stayed at Paul and Bertie's house, then slept in a car." Sammy took a couple of deep breaths.

"Oh, Sammy. I'm so thankful that you're home. And that you're ok?" Emily rubbed his back, then wiped her eyes and nose.

"Sure, I am." Sammy raised his shoulders and grinned at his parents.

"Thank God, you're home, Son. We've been so worried." Larry got up and crossed to the window trying to control his emotions.

"Yeah. Sure. I've been trying to get home. Etta Jean helped a me a yot."

Suddenly he remembered. "ETTA JEAN!" He jumped off his mother's lap. "Where is she? Etta Jean's daddy and mommy died, and her grandma forgot, and accidentally burned down the house that we saw. Her stepfather doesn't want her. She don't have no home, and I want her for my sister."

"Well, I don't think so." Larry moved back across the room to Sammy. "I saw a girl. She didn't look so good."

Sammy wiggled away from his father's arms. "Where is she? I gotta find her." He dashed out the front door. He could see her far down the sidewalk walking with her head down and dragging her backpack.

"Etta Jean. Etta Jean. Come back. Etta Jean," he yelled and ran after her. His father and mother hurried after him.

"Etta Jean, wait up. Etta Jean, please."

She stopped and looked back at them. Sammy saw that she was not crying, but she looked sadder than he had ever seen her.

Sammy ran and hurried to her. "Etta Jean, come home. Come back with me and be my sister."

His mother and father stopped a dozen feet from the homeless girl. She looked up at them with mute pleading in her eyes. His parents were not smiling. Sammy then knew his parents did not want her. He could tell Etta Jean knew it, too. She turned and started on down the street, her shoulders slumped, dragging her backpack.

Sammy stood there a moment stunned. Then he yelled crying at the same time. "Don't you want her, Mommy and Daddy? I want Etta Jean to be my sister."

His mother watched the young girl, but his father turned and started walking back to the house. "Come on, Sammy," he said.

"NO, DADDY. NOT WITHOUT ETTA JEAN!" Sammy yelled.

He ran to his mother, "Mommy, Etta Jean don't have no home. She doesn't have a place to sleep or nothin' to eat. She's fun, Mommy. She treats me nice, not like Per, uh, Sibyl. Etta Jean yaughs a yot. She took care of me and helped me get home." Sammy watched his mother's face. "Please, Mommy."

Emily stood still and looked at Sammy.

"I would have died if she hadn't helped me."

Sammy's mother still was looking at him.

"Mommy, I would never have come home if Etta Jean hadn't helped me. I would have died. The bus would have hit me if she hadn't pulled me back. Mommy, please."

Emily bit her lower lip, hesitated, then turned, and hurried after the young girl. "Etta Jean," she called. "Wait."

Etta Jean turned and faced her. Tears were rolling down the girl's cheeks. She said nothing.

Emily knelt down by Etta Jean and hugged her for a moment. Then Emily stood and looked at her husband. "Larry. Larry. Come back. We haven't thanked Etta Jean for saving Sammy's life and taking care of him. Thank you, Etta Jean." She knelt and hugged Etta Jean again. "Thank you, thank you, for taking care of our little boy."

Sammy ran to meet his father. "Daddy, I'd never got home if Etta Jean hadn't helped me. She kept me from being kilt, too. She pulled me back on the sidewalk when a bus was gonna hit me," Sammy grabbed his father's hand with both of his own. "Please, Daddy. She's awful nice, Daddy. Please. I woulda died if Etta Jean hadn't taken care of me. She doesn't have a home or any place to go. She's been sleeping in a cardboard box, but she doesn't have that anymore. Please let her stay with us. Please yet her be my sister." He started crying.

Sammy's father walked back He stopped several feet from Etta Jean. Sammy was afraid he saw just her torn sweat suit instead of her pretty face.

Sammy's mother stood up. Her mouth was open a little and her eyes were sad. She gave her husband a long, pleading look. "Please," she whispered. Larry looked at her and they stood looking at each other quietly for a few minutes. Sammy held his breath and tried to stop crying. Etta Jean stood with her head drooped and her shoulders slumped.

"This girl helped us get out son back." The breeze blew Emily's hair across her face. She pushed it back and waited a moment. "I've wanted another child for such a long time, Larry. I've always wanted a daughter," she said softly.

Sammy's tears stopped and he took a jagged breath, then held it again as he stared at his father.

"Please." Emily said. Sammy saw his mother beg his father with her eyes. She stood very still. Larry gave his wife a long, searching look.

Sammy had never seen Etta Jean look sadder. Although she had her head down, he could see her face like she wanted to cry but was too sad to even do that. Her shoulders were slumped so low that her arms hung down past her knees. Sammy watched his father stare at the girl for it seemed like several minutes.

Sammy rushed to him and looked up. He hit his clenched fists together several times. "Please, Daddy. Please."

Larry reached down and picked up his red haired son and held him close. He kissed his check and hugged him tightly.

"Daddy, I woulda died. And it's my bertday. All I wanted was a sister."

Larry put Sammy down and walked over to Etta Jean and Emily. He and Emily exchanged a long look, then he bent down and put his finger under Etta Jean's chin and lifted it up so he could see her face.

Her eyes were as pleading as a dog's eyes when it is being beaten.

Sammy saw different emotions on his father's face as he looked at the girl. Finally Larry said, "Come home with us, Etta Jean."

Etta Jean was quiet for a long moment. She wiped her tears from her cheeks with her sleeve and looked up at Larry. "You mean that?" Mister?"

Larry nodded and Emily smiled and nodded.

"You'd let me live at your house, Mister?" Etta Jean whispered so low that they could hardly hear her.

Sammy's father nodded and said smiled at Etta Jean.

Tears were dripping onto Emily's sweater. "Yes, oh, yes, Etta Jean." They all three stood there for a moment quietly while Sammy held his breath with his folded fists close to his chest. He stood without moving. Emily gently took the soiled and shabby backpack from Etta Jean, then took her hand.

The nine-year-old looked up at her with awe.

Sammy took a deep breath and wiped the tears from his freckled cheeks and nose with his jacket sleeve.

Standing up, Larry reached across and gently brushed the tears from Emily's cheeks. Then he took Etta Jean's other hand and smiled at her.

Suddenly Sammy started jumping up and down. "You're gonna be my sister, Etta Jean. You're really gonna be my sister." He ran ahead about ten steps then ran back to them. "You're gonna be my sister. You really are." He was so excited that he fell into an evergreen shrub in a neighbor's yard.

Without letting go of Etta Jean's hand, Larry reached across and pulled Sammy upright. They both laughed.

"Did the bush scratch Sammy, Mister?" Etta Jean asked.

Larry shook his head and exchanged a long, quiet look with Emily.

"How about calling me 'Daddy,'" he said.

Etta Jean laughed her deep-throated laugh, and Emily and Larry looked at her with surprise hearing her musical laughter for the first time.

Etta Jean's face brightened. She smiled. She looked at Sammy and laughed again. "They want me. They really, really, REALLY want me," she whispered in amazement.

Sammy turned around and began skipping toward home. "I'M HOME!" he yelled. "IT'S MY BERTDAY AND I'M HOME. IT'S MY BERTDAY AND I GOT A SISTER!" he yelled over and over. He clapped his hands. He'd run a few steps, stop, jump up and down, then run a few more steps all the time shouting.

Neighbors, hearing Sammy, came out their front doors.

Walking between Emily and Larry, Sammy saw Etta Jean's mouth was open and her eyes were wide. She looked up at the adults as though each was a 50-foot Christmas tree full of presents.

Sammy smiled at the three of them who smiled back. He had never seen Etta Jean with such a radiant smile and sparkling eyes. He laughed and continued to run back and forth, jump and yell. "I'M HOME! IT'S MY BERTDAY AND I GOT A SISTER!" He danced down the sidewalk and clapped his hands.

Neighbors—men, women, and children—came out of their houses. They heard Sammy's happy voice and saw Emily and Larry's smiles. They knew their missing neighbor boy was home safe and sound. They laughed and some came running and hugged Sammy. Then they hugged Emily and Larry. They cried. They laughed. All of them smiled. They said how glad they were that Sammy was now safe with his parents.

When Emily introduced them to Etta Jean they hugged her, too. They cried and smiled and laughed and hugged all of them.

"I never got so many hugs in my whole life," Etta Jean laughed.

Her face beamed. The tiredness left her. Her shoulders were straight and her chin was up. She gave a little skip and laughed her big deep throated laugh again.

Emily laughed through her tears. Larry and Sammy laughed. The neighbors laughed. Sammy was home safe! Etta Jean would be his sister! Sammy giggled and laughed and yelled with happiness all the way down the sidewalk.

They were all laughing and smiling with happiness.

And laughing with joy.

Especially Etta Jean.

ESPECIALLY ETTA JEAN!

(The End)

A sequel is planned.

NEXT BOOK

Will Etta Jean get to stay at Sammy's house?

Where will she sleep that first night? There is only a crib in the baby's room.

Will Etta Jean like Perfect Prissy Sybil? Will they get along?

When will she find her grandmother?

Will Emily and Larry adopt Etta Jean? What if they cannot find her birth certificate?

Will she ever see Grandma Jean and her grandfather?

Will Etta Jean become friends with Angela again?

The big question? Will she remain at Sammy's house?

If she does, will she and Sammy still remain friends?

A sequel is planned. The above questions and more will be answered.

If you would like something to happen in the next book, please write to the author and give her your opinion. She might use your idea in her book.

Her address is: Mrs. Reva Jo Gordon
P. O. Box 406
Flushing, MI 48433

About The Author

Reva Jo Kerns was editor of the award winning college newspaper, the Northwest Missourian, at Northwest Missouri State University, Maryville. After receiving a Bachelor of Science degree, she and classmate Roland Gordon were married. They attended the State University of Iowa. She taught English and business subjects in high schools at LeRoy, Iowa, Malvern, Iowa, Flushing, Michigan, and Platt Business College in St. Joseph, Missouri

After receiving a Master of Arts Degree from the University of Michigan, she became a librarian.

The Gordons have two children and four grandchildren.

Mrs. Gordon has had many articles, fiction, and one book published.

She has been named to *International Author And Writers' Who's Who* and others.

Printed in the United States
16195LVS00001B/184-276